BOUND TO THE ALPHA

ALPHAS IN HEAT BOOK ONE

OLIVIA T. TURNER

www.OliviaTTurner.com

Edited by Karen Collins Editing
Cover Design by Olivia T. Turner

BECOME OBSESSED WITH OTT

Sign up to my mailing list for all the latest OTT news and get a free book that you can't find anywhere else!

OBSESSED
By Olivia T. Turner
A Mailing List Exclusive!

When I look out my office window and see her in the next building, I know I have to have her.

I buy the whole damn company she works for just to be near her.

She's going to be in my office working under me.

Under, over, sideways—we're going to be working together in *every* position.

This young innocent girl is going to find out that I work my employees *hard*.

And that her new rich CEO is already beyond *obsessed* with her.

This dominant and powerful CEO will have you begging for overtime! Is it just me or is there nothing better than a hot muscular alpha in a suit and tie!

All my books are SAFE with zero cheating and a guaranteed sweet HEA. Enjoy!

Go to www.OliviaTTurner.com to get your free ebook of Obsessed

COME AND JOIN MY PRIVATE FACEBOOK GROUP!

Become an OTT Lover!

www.facebook.com/groups/OTTLovers

For my daughter,
Who's not allowed to read this book. Ever.

CHAPTER ONE

Ethan

"IT'S THIS FUCKING TOWN," RYLAN SAYS AS HE QUICKLY LACES up his boots. "There's like six girls in it and they're all either taken or we're related to them."

The fire alarm is blaring through the firehouse as the five of us throw on our gear and get ready to move out.

"That's a good thing as far as I'm concerned," Carter says as he gets behind the wheel. He closes the door and grins as he sticks his head through the open window. "Mates are more trouble than they're worth. We're better off without them."

"You're crazy," Westin says as he runs by, looking panicked. "I can't wait to find my mate and claim her tight little—Where the fuck is my coat?"

Our Chief, Blake, grabs Westin's coat from where he left it on the floor and tosses it to him. "You're not going to get a mate if you're all burned up. Keep your shit where it's supposed to go."

"Sorry, Chief," Westin says as he throws on his jacket and climbs into the firetruck.

I'm keeping my distance as I get ready. It never goes well for me when the subject of mates comes up.

"Let's move out!" Blake shouts as he climbs into the passenger's seat. "We got a hot one to put out."

Carter barely waits for us to climb into the truck before he hits the gas and flies out of the fire station.

There's silence for five wonderful seconds before the topic comes back up.

"You're quiet back there, Ethan," Carter says as he looks at me through the rearview mirror. "Are you on Team Mate or Team Masturbate?"

"So, that was you!" Westin snaps. "Stop clogging the drain with your spunk!"

Carter grins. "Never."

I hate talking about mates. My jackass inner grizzly bear was cool all morning, and now he's pacing around and about to take a furry temper tantrum. He's nasty when he gets like this—all agitated and ready to make my life miserable.

"I'm thirty-six years old," I tell them. "I'm done."

Rylan turns to me with his forehead all scrunched up. "What do you mean you're done? You can't be done when it comes to finding a mate."

"You heard him," Carter says with a winning smile on his face. "He's done. He's on team masturbate. We can be on team masturbate together." He turns around with his hand raised for a high-five.

I leave him hanging.

"I don't think so."

Rylan is laughing as he nudges my arm with his elbow. "Hear that, Ethan? You and him can masturbate together."

"All right," I say as I open the window. "I'll see you guys at the fire."

I grab onto the metal rails running along the roof and pull myself up with a grunt. We're barreling down a mountain road and I nearly get whipped by a tree branch as I climb onto the roof of the firetruck.

"Come on, guys," I hear Blake says as I pull my foot up. "You know how his bear gets."

I get comfortable on the roof and take a deep breath as I look at the stunning Montana mountains all around me. It's early morning and the sun is still rising, casting the vast sky in hues of pink and purple. We were just about to have our morning coffee at the station when the alarm went off.

I sigh as I try to settle my inner grizzly bear. It can be hard working with five bear shifters, especially when they start yammering on about their fated mates. The younger guys, Westin and Rylan, are convinced that their mates are right around the corner ready to rock their world, but an extra decade on this planet has shaken that belief in me. I still haven't found her, and believe me, I've looked.

I traveled the country for over a decade looking for my mate, but now I'm convinced that she's not out there. Maybe she died young, maybe she was never born, maybe it wasn't meant to be. Whatever happened, I've given up on trying to find her.

Three years ago, I moved to Blackcloud Point in Montana to settle down and become a firefighter. That's when I gave up the lifelong dream of finding her.

The only problem is, my bear hasn't.

He's not on board. In fact, he's more committed to finding her than ever.

And it's driving me crazy.

We're constantly at each other's throats. He hates that I'm not out searching for her every second of every day. Whenever I go to bed or crack open a can of beer to try and relax, he starts thrashing around like a rabid animal. The constant snarling and growling in my ear is really draining and it's starting to wear me down. I haven't slept well in months.

We're going to a fire, I say to him. *You have to chill.*

He responds with a furious roar as he charges to the surface and tries to claw his way out of me.

"*Fuck. You,*" I grunt as I flex my body, struggling to hold him back. It's like trying to stop a train, but somehow, I manage to push him back down.

I'm breathing heavily and I'm covered in a sheen of sweat as Carter turns the firetruck around the bend.

You have to stop that shit, I tell my grizzly. "She's not out there. We've looked everywhere."

I can feel him baring his teeth as he snarls at me.

Fated mates. It's such a load of bullshit.

Whoever said there was one girl destined for each bear shifter didn't know what they were fucking talking about. There's five of us here that are proof of that. Not one of us have found our mates. Even Blake, and he's fifty-two. If that's not proof that fated mates are bullshit, then I don't know what is.

I close my eyes and try to ignore the livid bear who is trying to hack and shred his way out of me and instead try to focus on the fresh mountain air that's running through my brown hair.

I *love* Montana and I'm having a blast working as a fireman with the guys in the truck down below.

But this is ruining everything. My stubborn bear is ruining everything.

He won't stop, and I don't know how to handle it.

The smell of smoke hits my nose as we get closer to the fire.

I open my eyes and see it snaking into the sky in the distance. It's coming from a two-story office building on the edge of town that's engulfed in flames.

I grin, expecting my bear to shrink down in fear like he always does when I'm near a fire, but the furry fucker doesn't even give me that satisfaction. He's as alert and focused as ever.

Buried in the thick heavy smoke is a sweet smell that suddenly sneaks through and hits me *hard*. My core clenches as a dump of adrenaline surges through my veins. It's a scent I've never smelled before, but it's so familiar. My body knows it intimately.

I breathe in deeply through my nose, trying to get as much of it as I can. It's faint and barely detectable, but it cuts through me like a thousand knives. It sears its way down my throat like battery acid. It scalds and burns my insides, but it feels so fucking good.

My bear starts raging inside like never before. He's acting like a mad dog as he thrashes around and bounds for the surface, desperate to get out. I drop to my hands and knees and scream out in frustration as I struggle to hold him in.

The nasty beast shreds his way to the surface until my arms are swelling up and my teeth are aching as my canines extend and sharpen.

I roll onto my back and grit my teeth as I fight him.

"*Fuck. Off. Cocksucker,*" I hiss as I squeeze my entire body, trying to pull him back in.

He's never been this strong. He's never been this bold. My grizzly has always been a primal beast who doesn't care that I'm trying to fit into society. He wants what he wants and right now he wants to get out and move closer to that scent.

But that sweet intoxicating scent is giving me strength as well and I manage to fight my bear back down. He gnarls and gnashes at me as I force him to return to the depths of my body.

With him taken care of for the moment, I turn back to the smell and breathe it in. The thick black smoke is overpowering the intoxicating scent as we get closer to the fire, but it's unmistakable…

It's *her*.

It's my mate.

My hands are shaking as I climb up to my feet, riding the firetruck like a surfboard. My whole body is tingling as I get closer.

"What the fuck is going on up there?" Rylan asks as he pokes his head out the window and looks up at me.

"I'm on Team Mate," I say as my heart pounds so hard that I'm worried it's going to vibrate out of my chest. "*That's* what's going on."

Carter turns the firetruck into the parking lot of the blazing building. Her scent is stronger than ever and my stomach drops when I realize that it's coming from inside of the burning building.

I leap off the truck before it stops and land in a summersault on the pavement. I spring back up and sprint toward the building as fast as I can. Past the parked cars, past the stunned people standing outside watching, past the billowing smoke and broken windows.

Without stopping, I take a deep breath and run into the burning building, ignoring the thick smoke that's searing my eyes and the hot flames that are licking my shoulders and back.

I have one focus.

Her.

I don't care if I come out covered in flames. I don't care if I take one step onto the sidewalk and burst into ash.

As long as she's safe, I'll die happy.

She's my only concern now. Her safety is all I care about.

My mate is in trouble and my protective instincts have taken over.

I just hope I'm not too late…

CHAPTER TWO

Chloe

I'M CHOKING ON THE THICK SMOKE AS I KICK THE WOODEN leg of my desk over and over again, but the stubborn thing refuses to break. My wrist is slick with blood and stinging like crazy as the metal handcuffs dig into my skin.

Come on!

I can feel the heat of the hungry flames from the other room as they spread toward me, stalking me as they get ready to feast on my flesh.

You're not dying like this. Come on, Chloe!

I give the thick oak desk leg a few more kicks, but it's useless. Nothing can kick through that strong wood.

My eyes are watering down my cheeks and I can't even open them as the thick gray smoke billows in through the open door.

My resolve begins to fade as I force my eyes open and

see the flames in the other room. They're traveling up the file cabinets that I was sorting through this morning and burning the files inside.

I guess I know now what I always suspected: Kirk Holdings Incorporated is a criminal organization.

The first time I suspected it was a few weeks ago when my boss, Aylwin Kirk, came walking into the office with a garbage bag full of loose bills. I was his personal secretary and I just pretended that what I saw was normal.

Why didn't I leave then?

I keep asking myself that question, but I know the answer. I had nowhere else to go. I'm only nineteen and I've already been on my own for two years.

Mr. Kirk paid well and I often turned a blind eye for that life-changing money. For most people, the paycheck wouldn't be life-changing, but for me it was. It was the difference between sleeping at a bus stop after my stepfather kicked me out and sleeping in a bed. I chose a bed. And this is where it got me.

Yesterday, the FBI came to visit when Mr. Kirk was away on business. They began asking me and some other employees questions about some missing cargo ships in the China sea. I had no idea what they were talking about, but Mr. Kirk seemed pretty agitated when I called him on the phone to tell him after.

I came into work early today like I always do and was surprised to see Mr. Kirk tearing up his office. It looked like a tornado had ripped through it.

"I thought you were in Hong Kong," I said to him as I put my coffee on my desk.

He looked on edge as he raced around his office, pulling out files and throwing them onto his desk.

"Something more important came up," he said as he

grabbed his laptop and broke it over his knee. I stared in shock as he tossed the pieces onto the floor.

"Anything I can help you with?"

His body stilled as he slowly turned to me. A shiver raced up my spine as his hard eyes locked onto mine. His eyes were normally bright green, but this morning they seemed to be glowing.

I took a step back as he grinned.

"Yes, actually. You can."

He leapt forward in a blur and grabbed my arm. I screamed and tried to yank it back, but his grip was unbreakable. He was incredibly strong.

Before I knew what was happening, he pulled me to the ground and handcuffed my wrist to the heavy desk.

"What are you doing?" I asked him as I stared at the metal chain in shock.

He just shrugged, like I wasn't even worth an explanation. "You know too much, Chloe." Without another word, he left and ran downstairs. A few minutes later, I started to smell the smoke.

My eyes are watering, but I'm forcing them open so I can keep an eye on the approaching flames. They start to spread along the cheap carpet as I kick the desk leg again and again, each strike gets weaker and weaker.

I'm just about to give up when I hear a siren in the distance.

Yes!

But the building is already in flames. It's going to take the firemen at least a few minutes to get here, park, set-up, and then come in. And I don't have a few minutes. By the time they get here, if they even enter the building, I'll be nothing but a pile of ash.

A pile of ash that accomplished nothing in her life. That

was tossed out of her house by her alcoholic mother and her druggie boyfriend. That never finished school. That has no friends. That has never had a boyfriend. Never been loved. Never even been kissed.

I'm going to die a virgin, having never felt the warm skin of a man pressed against mine or felt the loving protective feel of strong arms wrapped around me.

I'm going to die lonely and afraid. Which is pretty fitting after all, considering that's how I spent most of my life.

The flames reach the open door and start burning the wooden frame. I have seconds before they reach me, maybe a minute if I'm lucky.

I know I'm going to die. It hits me hard, and just as I'm about to wallow in my own self-pity, I hear thundering footsteps.

My back straightens and I force my eyes back open as I try to call out. The words don't come out thanks to the thick smoke that is filling my lungs. All I can do is hope and pray that the brave firemen get here in time.

The flames burst through the drywall and spread into the room. I wince when I feel the intense heat. My skin is slick with sweat, but it's doing nothing to cool me off.

The footsteps get louder and then I see him. He's *massive*. So big that his muscles strain against the big baggy firefighter uniform hung on his giant frame. His thick coat molds to his round biceps and is pulled tight against his enormous chest.

He's not wearing a helmet and I swallow hard when I see his face. It's hard with rough edges and a mean-looking scowl that softens when he lays his sexy brown eyes on me.

A jolt of something sizzles through me as he stands in

the flaming doorway and locks his territorial brown eyes on me with a heated stare.

I must look like shit. Sweaty, cheap dollar store make-up running down my face, hair a hot mess. It's ridiculous to think of what I look like right now when death is still a very serious possibility, but I can't help what goes through my head.

He stomps into the room on his thick powerful legs and kneels down in front of me.

"It's you…" he says in a deep growly voice as he stares at me in awe.

There's something about the way he's looking at me. Like he recognizes me or like he's seeing for the first time something he's been searching for and never quite found. I know I've never seen him before. I would have remembered that. You don't forget seeing someone like him.

His big hand is shaking as he slowly reaches out and cups my cheek. I lick my lips as an undeniable urge to kiss him rips through me. Maybe I just want to feel a man's lips on mine before I die, or maybe the smoke is making me hallucinate, but something is pulling me toward this man. Something strong and undeniable.

My body tingles as his hungry eyes roam over it. He spots the handcuff around my wrist and it seems to snap him out of his daze.

With a grunt, he punches the thick desk leg and it explodes into splinters. He catches the falling desk and throws it across the room as I stare in shock. *How the hell can he be that strong?*

I kicked that leg dozens of times and didn't even make a dent. *I must have loosened it for him.* But even as the thought passes through my mind, I know that it's not true.

He scoops me up in his big arms and cradles me to his

chest as he stands up. I can feel his heart pounding against my tingling body.

I'm staring up at his face as he holds me like I've always wanted to be held. It's better than I've ever dreamed of and I know that if I die now, I'll be dying happy.

His protective brown eyes lock onto mine and that heated gaze takes all the fear out of my body. His strong muscular arms are wrapped around me, holding me against his chest, and I know that nothing can hurt me while he's holding me like this. He won't let it.

"You're stunning," he whispers as he stares at me in awe. "You're the most beautiful thing I've ever seen."

He leans down and kisses me softly on the mouth. The edge of his hot tongue slides through my parted lips and my whole body melts when the tip touches mine.

His lips are soft, gentle, and I lean my chin up so he can deepen the kiss. He groans into my mouth as his hands tighten on my body. I've never been happier. But leave it to me to ruin it... I yank my mouth away and start coughing.

My sexy savior holds me tighter and starts moving. He sprints through one burning room after another as I squeeze my eyes shut and press my face against his chest. I focus on his pounding heart and not on the flames, not on the heat, not on the broken steps that he's leaping over.

He moves impossibly fast and before I can take another breath, we're outside in the crisp morning air. It's so fresh and even though my throat is burning, I choke down gulp after gulp of clean mountain air.

My eyes are watering, but I can see my coworkers in the parking lot arriving for work. I can see an ambulance approaching and firemen rushing around their truck as they set up their hoses.

"Ethan!" the oldest looking fireman shouts. "Are you fucking crazy?!?"

Ethan doesn't answer. He's too busy staring at my face like I'm the most gorgeous thing he's ever seen. Nobody has ever looked at me like this before and a part of me wonders if I actually died in the fire and am now waking up in heaven.

The hoses burst to life and the firefighters begin assaulting the flames with thick streams of water as Ethan carries me to the ambulance.

"Was she inside?" the male medic asks as he rushes to the back of the ambulance. "Let me have her."

His grip tightens on me and he snarls at the medic who's reaching for my arm. "She's *mine*."

The man's eyes widen and he jumps back in shock.

There's a female medic coming from the passenger's side.

"Her," Ethan grunts. "You stay back. This is *my* girl."

He's as possessive as a predator hovering over his meal. The look in his eyes is so primal and savage, and I know he can't help it. There's something feral in the way he's holding me in such a dominating and territorial way, but I like it. It's turning me on to see this man go wild over me. Like one look at me has erased any shred of civilization in him and replaced it with pure primal instinct.

The male medic backs away as the female medic opens the back doors to the ambulance. She quickly grabs an oxygen tank as Ethan places me on the gurney.

"No!" he snaps when she goes to put the mask on me. "I'm doing it."

She's about to protest, but when she sees the serious-ness on his face, she quickly hands it over.

For such a big man, he's extremely gentle as he puts

the mask on my face and wraps the string around my head.

"Just breathe," he says softly as he kneels in front of me. He turns the tank on and it's like ice in my burning lungs.

He stares into my eyes and breathes in and out deeply with me. I feel lightheaded with him so close, but I'm not entirely sure if it's from the oxygen, the smoke inhalation, or from his gorgeous brown eyes that seem to be staring into my soul.

I'm more than attracted to this man. It's running deeper.

It's not just the lure of a physical attraction or the excitement of lust. It's like I'm looking at my other half. Like our two cores are being pulled together and we're both helpless to stop them.

Andy the office creep comes over to check on me. "Are you okay, blue eyes?" he asks from the entrance to the ambulance. He's always calling me blue eyes and touching my shoulders even though I've repeatedly asked him not too.

Ethan whips his head around and growls at him. His eyes flash a golden color and he pulls his lips back and bares his teeth.

"Whoa," Andy says as his face pales as white as his shirt. He backs away with his hands up.

I grin as I turn back to my savior. His muscles are flexed and he's breathing heavily like he's trying to keep himself under control. He looks like a wild animal, but instead of being afraid, I'm even more intrigued.

My fingers are tingling as I reach up and touch his hard face. He instantly calms down and I love that I can soothe the monster in him.

"Can I check her now?" the male medic asks.

"No!" Ethan grunts. He grabs the doors and slams them closed, leaving us alone inside the ambulance, just how I like it. "It's okay," he says to me in a softer voice. "I have first aid training."

I pull off the mask and stare into his eyes as he gently checks my body.

My mind is racing as his big hands tenderly examine my neck.

"What was that kiss back there?" I ask him.

His eyes dart up to mine and we stare at each other for a long moment.

"I didn't know if we were going to make it," he says in a soft voice that makes the heat swirling through me settle between my legs, "and I couldn't die without tasting your lips. Did you not like it?"

"No," I quickly say. "I mean yes. I mean no… umm. What was the question?"

His hand slides around to the back of my neck and he pulls me in for another taste. My eyes close as his lips press against mine.

"*Mmmmm*," I moan as my mouth opens and I feel his hot tongue slide into it. His strong hand is wrapped around the back of my neck, holding me in place as my body melts.

He pulls away too soon and my lips are still in the air as my eyes slowly open. My body is burning with need for more of him.

"Did you like that?" he asks as he stares at my parted lips. "That was the question."

I swallow hard as I stare into his gorgeous brown eyes.

"I'm not sure," I say as I lick his taste off my lips. "Can you try one more time?"

He grins and kisses me deeper...

CHAPTER THREE

Ethan

THE SWEET TASTE OF MY MATE IS FILLING MY MOUTH AND
driving my bear mad as I make out with her. Her lips are
as soft as peaches and taste even better.

My cock has never been harder and it's burning with
every delicious second that goes by. All I can think about is
how good it's going to feel when I sink my big dick into
her tight little pussy. I'm imagining how soft and wet and
warm it's going to be as I hold her tight against me and
explore her sweet mouth with my tongue.

I can't believe I gave up on finding this girl. I hate to
say it, but my bear was right. I deserved all the shit he
gave me. If I knew she was going to be this fucking spec-
tacular, I would have slapped my old self too and then
continued looking for her.

She moans when I pull away from her mouth and lean
back to get another look at her. This is torture. I don't

know whether to taste her or to stare at her. They're both equally good.

My girl has long brown hair pulled back into a ponytail and the most vibrant blue eyes I've ever seen. She's as beautiful as an angel and I still can't believe she's real.

For the first time in months, my bear is calm and silent inside me. He's watching her in awe as well. It won't take long for him to begin harassing me to claim her pussy and put my mark on her neck, but for now, he's just reveling in her beauty, just like I am.

My hands are still on her thick body and they're not going anywhere anytime soon. Once I touched her curvy body, my hands haven't left. I don't know how I'm going to gain the strength to remove them. This is where they belong and I have a lot of lost time to make up for.

"Ethan." Her lips curl up into a smile as she says my name for the first time. I can't resist. I kiss those smiling lips again and press my tongue in deeper until she's moaning into my mouth and my hard dick leaks pre-cum down my thigh.

"What's your name?" I ask when I pull away. I need to know.

"Chloe," she says. "Chloe Webb."

"Chloe," I whisper, loving the way it feels on my tingling lips. "Chloe my mate."

"Your what?" she asks with a giggle.

"Nothing," I whisper. "We'll get to that later."

There's a pounding on the door of the ambulance and I push it open with a growl. If it's that creep who called her blue eyes I'm going to be in some serious trouble. I didn't like the way he looked at *my* girl and if he's back sniffing around my property, I'm going to have to tear his fucking throat out.

"Oh," I say in surprise when I see the Chief standing there. "Hi, Blake."

He looks at me and then looks at Chloe. My bear starts rumbling and pacing around inside. He doesn't like Blake looking at her even though he's the fire chief and a good friend. To be honest, I don't like it either, but I'm not about to start a fight with one of the closest people in the world to me over an innocent look.

"I see your bear found what he's looking for," Blake says as he turns back to me.

I nod. "He did. And I found what I needed."

He studies my face as he rubs his jaw with the salt and pepper beard on it. "Good. The fire is out and we're moving out soon. Rylan and Carter are almost done securing the building."

"All right."

"What about her?" he asks. "Miss, would you like to go to the hospital to get tested further?"

"I already checked her," I snap. There's something about him talking to her that I don't like. I've never been so possessive of anything in my life before, but anyone going near her, talking to her, or even looking at her is sending me spiraling off the deep end. I can't control it. "She's fine and she's staying with me."

Blake's eyes harden when they snap back onto mine. I can sense his inner polar bear getting pissed over the tone of my voice and he starts breathing a little heavier.

"I asked *her*," he answers with a warning in his tone.

That's the problem. I don't like him talking to her.

"It's okay," Chloe says. The sweet angelic sound of her voice soothes me and I take a deep breath, wondering why the hell I was ready to fight my oldest and closest friend. "I feel fine. I can stay with Ethan for a bit."

Blake takes a deep breath and nods. "Fine. Be on the truck in ten minutes."

He closes the door and I'm on her once again, kissing her and making her mine.

"Shouldn't we be going?" she asks after we've been kissing for an eternity. My cock is aching and my balls are so full and heavy that they feel like they're going to burst if I don't get some relief soon.

It's torture, but I pry my hands and lips away from her and carry her to the truck.

"Hey, blue eyes," that little prick says as we pass him outside. "Where are you going? Want to hang out?"

My arm darts out and I grab him around the neck with an impenetrable grip. His hands fly up to my wrist, but I'm not letting go until he gets the message loud and clear.

"This is *my* girl now," I hiss into his face. "You touch her and I'll take your hand. You look at her and I'll take your eyes. You talk to her and I'll take your life. You understand me?"

His face is turning purple as he opens his mouth to answer, but nothing comes out. I'm choking the words out of him.

"Do. You. Understand. Me?" I growl.

He nods his head up and down as best he can. "Good."

I throw him back and he slams into a parked car as he chokes in panicked breaths of air. Everyone from her company is staring at me in shock, but I'm glad. I want all of them to know what happens if they try to step foot on my territory. And Chloe is now my territory.

"I guess he's on Team Mate after all," I hear Rylan say as I grab onto the firetruck and climb up to the roof while I have Chloe clutched to my chest.

I guess I am.

Carter turns the truck on and it begins to rumble under us. He pulls out of the parking lot and Chloe grips onto me as she looks around with fear.

"Don't be scared, peaches. I got you. I'll always have you."

She settles down as the truck turns onto the road. I pull her onto my lap and hold her tight as she looks at the burnt building as it gets smaller in the distance.

I have a million questions for her, but she's been through a lot and I don't want to put her through any more hardship. But there's one question I need to know the answer to.

"Who handcuffed you to the desk?"

My blood is boiling and my bear is on edge as we wait for the answer. I'm going to take the life of whoever is responsible. I'm going to *end* them.

I'm squeezing my hands into fists and clenching my jaw just thinking about it.

She looks up at me with her tender blue eyes and the anger in me settles for the moment. I tuck a strand of her brown hair behind her ear and force out a smile. "It's okay. You can tell me. I'm going to protect you now, Chloe. I'm on your side."

She takes a deep breath and I know that she believes me. "It was my boss. Aylwin Kirk."

My bear lets out a low growl that I feel vibrating throughout my chest. She must feel it too because I see her eyes narrow in confusion.

"Why was he trying to kill you?" I can barely talk with the intensity of my wrath building inside. I need to find this Aylwin Kirk and show him just how violent my grizzly bear can get.

But it's not like it's going to be as easy as putting that creep outside in line.

It's going to be much harder. And much more deadly.

Because Chloe's scent wasn't the only smell I recognized in that burning building. The scent of something far more sinister was swirling around as well…

"I don't know," she says. "He just handcuffed me and left me to die."

I hold her tighter as she thinks about it.

We drive down the quiet mountain road as the sun washes its heat down on us from above.

"I'm pretty sure he's running a criminal enterprise. The FBI was in the office yesterday, so maybe he was trying to tie up loose ends? I guess I was one of them."

"Where can I find this Aylwin Kirk?"

She shakes her head as she looks up at me with watery eyes. "Don't go find him. *Please*. Just stay here with me. I don't want you to get hurt."

I kiss her forehead and nod, even though I know I can't let this go. He tried to kill my mate and I can't let that slide. I must make it right by ending his life.

But it won't be easy.

The scent that I picked up, the scent of Aylwin Kirk, was that of a dragon shifter.

And those fuckers *always* put up a fight.

CHAPTER FOUR

Ethan

MY POSSESSIVE BEAR IS GROWLING IN MY EAR AS I LET CHLOE go. He hates that I'm leaving her, even for a second.

No! Go back. Hold her. Claim her!

He's pacing around like a crazed animal in a cage, snarling and letting me know how furious he is with me.

Mark her. Now!

He doesn't speak in words, but his intention is *very* clear. I always seem to know just what he wants, and all he wants is her.

"I feel you, buddy," I whisper to him as I hurry over to the front of the truck and kneel down on the roof over the driver's side. "I love being near her too."

We're still driving along the quiet mountain roads as I grab onto the emergency lights with one hand and lean over.

"Oh shit!" Carter shouts when he suddenly sees me in

his window. He swerves the truck for a second and I immediately whip my head back to see if Chloe is okay. I really hate to leave her, especially on the roof of a moving firetruck, but she's fine. She's tucked beside the ladder in the roof indentation, so it's going to take a lot more than a swerve to knock her loose.

"Drop us off at my place, will you Carter?" I say to him.

Blake is in the passenger's seat shaking his head. "It's a workday, Ethan."

"I'm taking the day off."

Chief looks pissed, but I know it's not because I'm taking the day off. I think I've taken maybe one day off in the three years since I've been working at the station. And he knows if he calls me in for a fire, I'll be there to help, day off or not. This is about how I snapped at him back there.

"I'm sorry I bit your head off," I tell him and he lets out a big sigh.

"It's fine," he grunts. "I know you can't help it right now. Your bear is extra possessive over your mate because there's no mark on her neck, but if you ever growl at me like that again, I'll bite your fucking head off for real. Understand?"

Carter is snickering until I slap the back of his head.

"Got it, Chief," I say to Blake.

He nods then turns to Carter. "Drop them off at his place so he can mark his girl and we can all go back to normal."

"Thanks, Chief." I pull myself back up and turn to look at Chloe. When I see her sitting there with her brown hair flowing in the wind and a shy smile on her stunning face, I know that things will never go back to normal ever again. Not for me anyway.

She's changed *everything*. I'm already obsessed.

I study every inch of her face and body as I walk back to her. Her eye make-up has made a black mess on her round cheeks from when her eyes were watering from the smoke, but I can see past that to the beauty underneath. I can't wait to see her au natural with no make-up ruining her breath-taking features.

The wind is making her hair dance all around her and it looks alive with energy as I approach her. God, I just want to sink my hands into it and hold her while I thrust my still rock hard cock into her tight little pussy.

My bear groans inside as I think about all the dirty stuff I want to do with her. I want to take her in every position. I want to make her scream so loud that my eardrums explode. I want to pump every drop of my hot cum into her little cunt until her womb is drenched in my seed with my baby growing inside of it.

"I should go home," she says as I sit back down behind her.

My heart nearly breaks from her words. It actually physically hurts.

"No," I say as I wrap my arms around her and pull her back into my chest where I can keep her safe. "You're staying with me."

"But, I'll be a burden."

I gently take her chin and turn her face until she's looking into my eyes. "You'll never be a burden to me. Understand?"

She nods and I feel my whole body shiver as those stunning blue eyes gaze up at me.

"You're coming to my place," I say in a commanding

voice that leaves no room for any buts. "This Aylwin guy could come and get you and I can't let that happen. I want you at my place where I can keep an eye on you. You're going to stay with me and I'll keep you safe."

She shifts a little closer into my embrace and I squeeze my big arms around her to let her know just how good I'm going to take care of her.

"But for how long?" she asks with a hint of worry in her voice. "I can't stay at your place forever."

She can and she will. She doesn't know it yet, but she's never leaving. I can't allow it. There's no way I'm going to let my mate go off into the world without her two thousand pound furry bodyguard by her side and looking out for her. She's the most precious thing in the world to me and my bear, and she's going to find out just how possessive a pair we are.

"Don't worry about a thing," I whisper to her as I run my fingers through her hair and massage her scalp. "Just sit back, relax, enjoy the mountain view, and know that I'll take care of you properly."

She sighs and melts into me as we look at the stunning mountains in the distance. My cock is still rock hard and raging in my pants—I'm not sure if the beast is ever going to be soft again—and Chloe lets out a little whimper when her back presses against it. She doesn't get upset or jump out of my arms when she feels how thick and hard my shaft is. Chloe just pretends not to notice and stays pressed against it, which makes my bear crazy. Hell, it makes me crazy too. A fresh stream of pre-cum oozes out the tip and drips down my thick veined shaft. Luckily, it's not going to leak through my firefighter pants and get her all wet.

With her pressed against my cock, I start to realize how

badly I need some relief. My balls are aching and so full that they feel like they're going to explode.

Her delicious scent is swirling in my nose and making me all light-headed and the feel of her curves under my palms are just... fuck... there are no words to describe it. It's pure heaven.

"You don't mind me staying with you?" she asks in a small timid voice that sends a jolt straight to my cock. "We just met."

How can I tell her that we're mates and even though we just met, it already feels like I know her intimately? How can I tell her she's mine and I won't ever let her go?

"Do you believe in love at first sight, Chloe?"

She chuckles and then turns around to see if I'm serious. I am.

"Love at first sight?" she says as she stares at me in disbelief. "I'm afraid to look in a mirror right now. There's ash in my hair, I reek of smoke, my mascara must be a mess, my hair is a nightmare. What's wrong with you that you can fall in love with this?"

"What's wrong with you that you can't see how utterly perfect you are?"

She laughs and then turns back around while shaking her head. "I think you inhaled too much smoke."

I just hold her even tighter and kiss the top of her head. "I think I'm finally awake for the first time in my life."

Carter turns the firetruck onto my street and it won't be long before she's in my place. My bear keeps stalking around and is still unable to relax. I know how he feels. I'm torn.

I *need* to hunt down and kill this dragon shifter like I need to breathe. Any threat to my mate must be eliminated immediately, but there's another competing need coursing through my veins as well.

I *need* to explore her young ripe body and claim every inch of her. I *need* my cock in her cunt and my mark on her neck.

The firetruck comes to a stop in front of my place. It's a lakefront house overlooking the mountains and surrounded by tall trees. I've always loved it, but now I'm seeing it through new critical eyes. It's too small. It's only got one bathroom. I'm terrified that Chloe won't be happy here.

"Is that your house?" she says as she leans up to get a better view. Her back leaves my hard cock and I almost grab her and pull her back down onto it. I squeeze my hands into fists to stop myself.

"Yeah. Do you like it?"

I can't breathe as I wait for her answer.

"I love it. It's so cute."

I'm so relieved that I can't wipe this goofy smile off my face as I help her climb down from the truck.

The boys are sticking their heads out of the windows and I nearly growl at them to stop looking at my mate, but I hold it back. They know she's my mate and that she's off-limits. They're smart enough to know not to test me in that area. I know that, but I'm still learning to handle all of these new possessive feelings that are taking over.

"One more for Team Mate," Westin says with a smile. "You're all on your own now, Carter."

Carter is shaking his head. "It's a damn shame too. He had such potential."

The firetruck starts to roll and Chloe waves at them. "Thanks for everything, guys."

"No problem," Blake says as he waves back at her.

"You just take care of our boy. And make sure he comes up for some fresh air once in a while."

The truck rolls down the road and we're finally alone.

"What did he mean by coming up for fresh air?" she asks with a sparkle in her eye.

I shrug. "Who knows?"

But I do know. And she's going to find out soon enough.

We head inside the house and I lock the door behind us while she walks around my place. I would take some wooden boards, a hammer, and some nails to barricade her in so she could never leave if I had my way, but I don't want to freak her out too much.

Every instinct I have is urging me, *begging* me, to keep her trapped in here. It's a new side of me. A dark, possessive side that I don't know if I can control.

She looks into my bedroom and my whole body aches.

I guess I'm about to find out just how much control I have…

CHAPTER FIVE

Chloe

THIS IS THE BEST HOT SHOWER OF MY LIFE. I LET OUT A LITTLE moan as I close my eyes and let the water wash over my face.

It feels so good, but I can't concentrate on the water for long. Not with Ethan in the other room. I can't stop thinking about the way he looks at me and fantasizing about him coming in here and seeing me with nothing on but my blushing cheeks.

My clit is throbbing and my pussy is aching with need.

Don't do it… I warn myself.

But my hand doesn't listen. It's sliding down my wet stomach and I swallow a moan as my fingers glide through my wet folds. This is a bad idea. Ethan is right outside.

I know I should stop, but I can't seem to stop myself. I can't help it. My pussy is *burning*.

Maybe it's the smell of his soap or knowing that his big sexy body was naked in this very spot a few hours ago. Or maybe it's knowing that he's so close by, but once my fingertip starts rubbing my clit, I know I'm not going to be able to stop until I let out some of this pent-up sexual desire with an orgasm.

My forehead is pressed against the cold tiles and my mouth is open wide as I rub my engorged clit in tight little circles. I can still feel how hard his cock was pressed against my back. I wanted to turn around and pull it out to see if it was as long and thick as it felt.

What are you doing, girl?

Fuck… I've never been this turned on before. Ever.

I don't do stuff like this. This is not me. I'm a virgin who's barely ever touched herself and now I'm masturbating in a stranger's shower. What has gotten into me?

The throb between my legs intensifies as I slide my fingertips to my hole to feel how wet I am. I wonder if Ethan would like my naked body. I wonder if he would mind that I'm a virgin. Would he mind that I've never been touched by another man before?

I can't stop thinking about him. I feel myself being pulled to him like the sun pulling on the earth. He's my world now and I don't understand it. I don't understand any of this.

"*Oh, fuck,*" I whimper as I return to my clit. I'm imagining that it's Ethan's fingers instead, feeling how soft and wet I am, feeling how much I want him.

A big sexy fireman saved my life. Of course I have a crush on him. Any other normal girl would. But this? I don't know if this is normal.

I wipe the steam away from the glass of the shower stall and look around the bathroom. There are signs of him everywhere. His towel hanging on the back of the door. His razor. His toothbrush. I imagine his sexy lips wrapped around it and I start rubbing myself harder as the heat intensifies within.

I'd laugh if I wasn't so turned on. This is ridiculous. I'm masturbating to a freaking toothbrush.

Oh, fuck… How can I go on without this man?

He's letting me stay here with him now, but what happens after tonight? What if they find Mr. Kirk and arrest him? Then what? I go back to my lonely, pathetic apartment and my sad little life? Jobless, friendless, moneyless, manless? I can't. I want to stay here. Forever.

This is what I want. I want Ethan. I want to be his.

I bite my bottom lip and fight back the moans that are coming with increased frequency and strength as I fantasize about staying here and having a life with him. I rub harder and faster as I picture my stomach growing with his child. I see a baby in his muscular arms. A smile on his face as he sees the life we've built together.

I imagine the nights full of passion and energy as he climbs on top of me and sinks his hard cock into my burning pussy and it sets me off. Big time.

The heat comes blooming up inside me in fierce waves that get more intense by the second. My whole body is tight with the need to release as I keep rubbing my clit and fighting back the screams that are desperate to get out.

With a cry, the orgasm rips through me and shakes me to my trembling core. I crumple against the cold tiles and gasp as my body shakes and writhes around my hand. My legs clamp shut and my eyes squeeze closed as the relentless hot water rains down on my twisted shivering body.

I'm breathing heavily and trying to regain my composure when I realize that I cried out loud. *No!* How loud was I? Did he hear?

I start to panic as I wonder if he heard me masturbating in his shower. He's going to think I'm insane. He's going to kick me out.

I told you it was a bad idea! Why didn't you listen?!?

My chest tightens with nerves as I stare at the door. It suddenly bursts open and Ethan storms into the bathroom, shameless and dominant, with a possessive look on his face like he owns me.

"What are you doing in here?!?" I shout as I quickly cover up my private parts with my hands. The steam from the shower is fogging up the glass, which should hide everything from him but my thick curvy silhouette.

"I heard you crying out," he says in a firm voice. It sends another tremble vibrating through my clit and my pussy begins to ache again with his eyes on me.

I grab onto the glass door and slide it open just far enough to stick my head out.

"I wasn't crying out," I lie. "It was a scream. I... uh, almost, slipped."

He stands there shamelessly staring at my body through the foggy glass and a small part of me wishes it wasn't foggy so he could see everything.

"So, can I have a... some privacy?" I ask him.

I don't know why I can't ask him for what I really want, but that's never been me. I've always been shy with my body and I've never been direct or aggressive with my sexual needs. Fearful yes, but direct no.

My eyes roam down his big hard body as I wait for his answer and I nearly gasp when I see the hard long outline of his big cock. It's sticking straight up against the inside of his jeans like it's about to tear through the thick fabric. Is he hard like that for… me?

I can't take my eyes off it. My mouth waters as another deep moan falls from my parted lips.

Ethan raises his nose and inhales deep. His brown eyes sparkle when he smells something he likes.

"I don't think you slipped," he says as he starts walking toward me with all the confidence in the world. "I think you were touching yourself."

I gulp as he stands in front of me. This man is *massive*. He towers over me and makes me feel so tiny, which I didn't think was possible. It's such a turn on. Everything about him is a turn on from his big feet to his messy brown hair that somehow looks incredibly sexy.

"Were you touching yourself in my shower, peaches?"

I can't move under his hungry gaze. I'm like a cobra hypnotized by this charmer. I don't scream for him to leave. I don't close the shower door. All I do is breathe heavily as I stare up at him.

"You can tell me the truth," he says. "I won't be mad. Were you touching that soft little pussy of yours in my shower?"

How did he know? Was I that loud?

I don't know how to answer, but I don't want to lie to him.

"Yes." The word comes out on its own. I didn't say it. Something deep inside of me did.

His heated eyes never leave mine. "You don't ever have to touch yourself again. That's your mate's job."

I can barely talk. "My… mate…?"

He grabs the door with his big hand and yanks it open.

I gasp as I back up into the corner of the shower and

try to cover myself. It's hard with all of my curves and only two tiny hands to cover them all.

His jaw tightens as he gets an eyeful of my big hips.

"You don't have to hide yourself from me," he says with a low growl in his voice. "Your body was made for my eyes."

My mouth opens, but nothing comes out as he steps into the shower fully clothed. The water pours down onto his tight black t-shirt and faded jeans, but he doesn't seem to notice or if he does, then he doesn't care in the least.

Our eyes lock on one another as he slowly reaches toward me and takes my wrist.

My whole body is tingling as he gently pulls my hand away from my chest. My naked breasts tumble down and he moans as he looks at them. God, my nipples are so hard. They're aching from his sexy gaze. He sees how hard they are and he sucks in a breath and holds it in.

I'm the one that removes my hand from where it's covering my pussy. I want him to see how wet he makes me.

His eyes darken with need as he pulls them away from my naked tits to take a look at the soft curls on my pelvis and throbbing pussy lips underneath.

The water is drenching him. His hair is wet, but somehow it looks even better. The water runs over his face and tempting lips as he stares down at the pussy I kept safe for him.

"Your body is beautiful," he says in a deep voice that sends tremors aching through me. "I knew my mate would have curves."

I don't know why he keeps calling me his mate, but I kind of like it. Almost as much as I like having his eyes on me.

His big hands come up and he cups my wet naked breasts and rubs his thumbs over my nipples, making them even harder. My heart is pounding and I can't seem to think straight with his eyes and hands on me like this.

"That cry that came out of your sexy lips," he growls. "Was that you cumming?"

I nod my head up and down as I stare into his dark eyes. "Yes."

He drops to his knees and I gasp. His shirt and jeans are completely soaked as he stares up at me.

"You're in my house and any moans that come out of your sexy little mouth are going to be caused by me. Got it?"

I nod.

With his big hands, he grabs my legs, picks me up, and throws my thick thighs over his round shoulders. I can't breathe. My naked pussy is spread open in front of his face.

He stares at it for a long moment then gives it a soft kiss.

His lips on mine send lightning shooting through my body. I've barely recovered when he dives in and *devours* me.

He doesn't start slow or tenderly, he eats my pussy like he's got seconds to live. I cry out even louder than before as his hot glorious tongue moves through my folds and pushes deep into my hole. His lips wrap around my swollen clit and he sucks it mercilessly as my back flattens against the cold tiles and whimpers come flying out of my mouth.

I'm breathing heavily and loving every excruciating moment as I look down at his beautiful body. His wet shirt is plastered to his back and I can see every tight muscle rippling and clenching as he buries his face between my trembling legs.

An orgasm comes rushing forward even faster than before. The scream that rips from my lungs is deafening as my whole body combusts. His grip on my ass tightens and his tongue moves even faster as I coat his relentless mouth with my virgin cream.

The back of my head is pressed against the hard tile and I'm moaning, whimpering, choking out breaths as he keeps going and going and going...

...giving me one hard orgasm after another...

Until I'm putty in his hands...

CHAPTER SIX

Ethan

THIS LITTLE PUSSY IS SO FUCKING SWEET. SHE'S GOT TO BE A virgin.

Her body is still shuddering from the last orgasm, but I can't stop eating her out. I'm not ready to leave and as long as she keeps creaming out this sweet syrup, I'm going to stay here and drink it up.

Her legs are trembling over my shoulders and every so often, her thick thighs clamp around my head when I hit the right spot. My palms are gripping her soft ass cheeks as she makes the sexiest moans and cries imaginable. I'm so fucking hard and every time she moans my name, I nearly cum in my pants like a damn teenager.

The water from the shower has soaked my clothes straight through and I'd take everything off if I could leave this delicious spot even for a second, but I can't.

I pull my head back just to see how pink her hot little

pussy is. "*Fuck*," I moan. I didn't know that shade of pink existed. I run my thumb up her soft folds and then rub her clit in tight circles as I look up at her.

Her ripe young tits are hanging over my head, swaying and bouncing in the most inviting way. Her hard nipples are almost as pink as her wet cunt is and my mouth waters with the need to taste every inch of them. But one thing at a time. Her spread pussy is in front of my face and I'm not ready to move on just yet.

I dip my head back in between her soft thighs and tease her little crease with my tongue. Her fingers slide into my wet hair and she grips it in fistfuls. Another rush of warm juice comes out and I greedily lick it up and spread it over my lips and chin. I want to be tasting her for days. I want to walk around and smell her cunt wherever I go.

Her little trembles turn into violent shakes as I suck on her clit again. Her back arches off the tiles and then slams back onto it as she screams my name. "*Fuck, Ethan!*" I lick her harder as she flies over the edge, giving me a fresh load of cream. Her warm pussy pulses against my chin as she shakes like she's having a seizure up there. Her grip on my hair tightens and I think I might be bald by the time we finally leave this shower.

"How many orgasms is that, peaches?" I ask her when the worst of the shaking is over.

She covers her eyes with her hand as she breathes heavily. I'm looking up at her, but my eyes keep going to her voluptuous tits that bounce up and down with every heavy breath.

"I don't know," she answers in gasps and moans. "Four? Five? They're just blurring into one now…"

Only five? I can do a little better than that.

I've never done anything like this before. I'm a thirty-six-year-old virgin, by choice. I could have had loads of women throughout the years. I've had numbers and hotel rooms shoved in my hands, I've had women throw themselves at me and whisper the nastiest things in my ears. I've even woke up to a naked woman in my room, but I told her what I told all of the others: *I'm not interested*. I was never interested in anyone but my mate.

No other woman turned me on, so it wasn't hard to say no. They didn't tempt me at all. Sure, I thought they were pretty, some even sexy, but that didn't mean I wanted them.

I only wanted *her*.

My mate.

Chloe.

I didn't know her at the time, but she was the only girl who got me going. I'd lay awake at night and touch myself, thinking about how her pussy would feel on my mouth and clamped down around my cock. I'm happy to say it feels even better than how I imagined it.

"How about we go for double digits?" I ask her with a grin. "Although, you taste so fucking good, peaches. I don't know if I'll be able to stop at ten. We might have to go for triple digits."

I return to where I belong between her legs and give her long soft strokes of my tongue as my cock burns. My dick is so hard that it's unbearable.

With one hand on her ass holding her up, I reach down and fumble with my zipper. My dick is so long and hard that it takes a minute for me to pull it out. And when I do, it's a mess. I'm covered in so much pre-cum that it looks like I came all over myself.

My little peaches' moans have turned into whimpers as

I wrap my hand around my thick cream-covered shaft and start stroking.

It doesn't take long for me to go off. My balls tighten up, ready to explode as I stroke my big throbbing cock harder.

When it comes, it comes *hard*. I pull back from her cunt, grit my teeth, and let out a savage roar as I cum all over the shower floor.

The carnal sound sets Chloe off and she cums too. The intensity of both of us cumming rocks me to my core and my head drops back in bliss. The warm water from the shower is spraying on my face and I've never been happier than in this moment.

My huge load runs down the drain, but my cock is still rock hard and ready to fuck. Cumming doesn't do anything to relieve the intense need that I'm feeling. It just makes it worse.

Inside, my grizzly bear rumbles in disapproval. He was silent this whole time, finally happy with my actions, but he doesn't like or understand why my load is down the drain and not deep in her pussy and traveling to her womb right now. He starts huffing out angry breaths as he begins pacing around again. I'm going to pay for this over the next few hours, but right now I just try to ignore him and enjoy the feeling of my naked girl on top of me.

"Ethan…" she moans as her eyes close. "I can't…"

She looks spent. Exhausted. She'd fall down and collapse onto the tiles if I wasn't holding her up.

I don't want to stop, but my girl is done. We have all night to continue. Hell, we have our entire lives to pick up and continue from here.

Carefully, I bring down one trembling leg at a time. Her

whole body is shaking as the warm water washes over her. She can barely keep her eyes open as I hold her up.

I take her out, wrap her in a fluffy towel, and then quickly take off my wet clothes and toss then into the shower after I turn the water off.

"It's okay, peaches," I whisper to her as I pick her up and cradle her to my chest. "You're with your mate now. You have nothing to worry about." I kiss her forehead and she smiles even though I'm pretty sure she's already asleep.

I bring her into my bedroom and lay her on the bed. By the time I close the curtains and return to her, she's already in a deep sleep.

She's so fucking perfect. I can watch her sleep for days.

Her gorgeous face looks so angelic and peaceful. Even my furious bear calms down as I admire her beauty.

I lean down and give her a soft gentle kiss on her lips. She moans, but doesn't wake.

"I love you," I whisper as I cover her with my sheets. "Now and forever."

After laying out some fresh clothes that are going to be way too big for her, I close the door to let her sleep and return to the bathroom.

I take her clothes from the floor so I can wash the smokey smell out of them. I want to smell her intoxicating scent when I'm with her and the heavy smell of the smoke overpowers it.

My body freezes when I see her panties.

Shit. My cock is already aching again just knowing her sweet pussy was touching that fabric.

I can't help myself. I'm so weak when it comes to her.

With my heart pounding, I take them and put them to my nose, inhaling her delicious scent once again. I start jerking off and when I'm ready to cum, I bunch them around the tip of my cock and cum all over them.

"*Mmmmmm*," I moan as I melt against the wall.

I turn to jelly, but my cock doesn't soften.

It won't until I feel the soft walls of her fresh young pussy clamped around it.

Until then, I'm just going to have to suffer.

CHAPTER SEVEN

Chloe

I WAKE UP WITH A HEAVY MOAN. I WAS IN SUCH A DEEP SLEEP that it takes me a second to remember where I am, but when I feel the pulsing heat of complete and utter satisfaction flowing through my pussy, I remember. I'm with Ethan.

Man, that was unreal. A part of me thinks it must have been an incredible dream, but my pussy has never felt this good and satisfied, so I know it must be real.

There's a pile of clothes next to me and I smile when I see that he folded them nicely. He's a man who pays attention to the small details, which I love.

Details like folding, not details like size. I chuckle when I pick them up and see how enormous they are. There's no way they're going to fit, but unless I want to walk around his house naked, which I seriously consider for a split second, I'm going to have to try.

I slip on the gym shorts and pull the string as tight as I can until the waist is so scrunched up that it looks like a frill. I tie the string and laugh when I see that the shorts look more like pants on me. This guy is huge.

The shirt is equally ridiculously big, but I manage to tie the bottom into an 80's knot and stick my bare shoulder out of the head hole, so it looks kinda cute.

My hair was wet when I went to bed so I have a weird bumpy afro-thing going on. I quickly brush it out and wrap it up into a bun. I wish I had some make-up, but at least I look better than before. I was horrified to see what my watery eyes had done to my eye make-up before my shower. I looked like a goth kid who got caught in the rain. I guess that's what happens when you buy mascara at the dollar store. Oh, well. It was all I could afford.

When I'm looking as good as I'm going to get, I open the door and creep down the hall. Ethan is in the kitchen, listening to old rock music as he cooks.

I lean against the wall and take a moment to admire him as he moves around the kitchen like he belongs there. For a big hulking guy, he's very light on his feet and agile.

"I hope you're hungry," he says with his back to me. "I'm cooking up a storm."

I smile. How did he even know I was here?

"I'm starving."

He turns around with such a sexy smile that it makes my body shudder.

"Good," he says with a grin. "I like a girl with an appetite."

I have an appetite… for him.

"You look stunning," he says as he looks me over slowly from head to toe.

"I'm wearing quadruple XL clothes and my hair looks like a bird's nest in January. I'm hardly stunning."

He shakes his head as he skewers me with a heated look. "You're *stunning*."

His dominant voice leaves no room for argument. He says it like it's a fact and that's that. It's not open for discussion.

I smile shyly as I feel my cheeks start to blush. For once in my life, I do feel stunning. He's making me feel that way.

"Come sit," he says as he points to the granite island.

I walk over and sit on one of the barstools as I watch him move. "I'd offer to help, but it looks like I'd just get in your way."

"I love to cook," he says as he pulls some delicious smelling salmon out of the oven. "When the crew gets together at the station, I'm always the one to cook."

"So, what's on the menu today?"

He smiles as he shows me. "I didn't know what you liked, so I made a few things. Maple salmon or grilled veggie sandwiches for the main course. Sweet potato, arugula, and wild rice salad with ginger dressing for the side, and of course..." I wait in anticipation as he opens the cupboard and pulls out a bag of potato chips. "...chips."

My mouth is hanging open in shock. I've never eaten like this before. Ever.

"You made all of this while I was sleeping?"

"It was either that or pace up and down the hallway, driving myself insane while I waited for you to wake up."

I laugh. "I'm glad you chose the food."

He grins as he takes out two plates.

I'm supposed to be at work right now. I have a peanut butter and jelly sandwich under my desk. Did I fall into some sort of an alternate reality or something? How did I get here, but more importantly, how can I stay?

"The sandwich looks incredible with some salad," I say with my mouth already watering.

He makes me a plate and adds some of the salmon with it. "You have to try some of the salmon too. I caught it myself."

"You like to fish?"

He shakes his head. "No."

"Then how did you catch it?"

A flash of panic crosses his face. "I meant at the grocery store. So, Chloe. Are you from Montana?"

I start to tell him about myself. I'm usually pretty candid with personal details, but for some reason, everything comes flooding out when I talk to him. I tell him all about how I left home when I was seventeen.

My mother was always drunk and I got into a huge fight with her druggie boyfriend. He slammed me against the wall—I leave that part out since I think he might storm out of here and run to Atlanta to break Roger's skull if I tell him—and I knew that it wasn't a good place for me to be anymore. I left the next day and got on a bus to Montana. I didn't even know what Montana was, just that it was the next bus leaving.

I rented a small room over a nice couple's garage for three hundred bucks a month and got a job working for Aylwin Kirk. It was all going okay until he tried to kill me.

He listens so closely, absorbing every word that comes out of my mouth with interest. He asks questions and I can tell that he wants to know everything about me. Kinda like I want to know everything about him.

I watch in awe as he devours the huge helping of salmon and polishes off three sandwiches, the big bowl of salad, *and* the bag of chips. This man has a giant appetite and not a lick of fat on him. He's all big shredded muscle.

"What about you?" I ask him after I finish my bite of the delicious food. "Were you born in Blackcloud Point?"

"No," he says as he scoops another heaping helping of salmon onto his plate. "I moved here three years ago, and before that, I was traveling the country for ten years. Just drifting from place to place."

"Were you trying to find yourself?"

"Yeah," he says softly. "Kind of like that. I was trying to find the rest of me."

I smile shyly. "Did you find it?"

He stares right at me with such intensity that it makes my toes curl. "I did now. Yeah."

He tells me about his parents back east and how he got the job at the fire station. I can tell that this stoic and reserved man doesn't open up to just anyone like this. I feel honored and special that he's opening up to me.

By the time we're finished lunch, my crush on him has intensified significantly. I can't keep my eyes off him.

"Can I ask you a question?" I ask as he's putting the dishes in the dishwasher. I tried to help but he wouldn't let me.

"Anything."

"Why do you keep calling me your mate?"

He sucks in a breath and looks a little nervous. "Did I say that out loud?"

"Multiple times."

He looks at me for a long moment and it feels like he's seeing more than just the surface level stuff. I can't explain it.

"I feel a pull to you, Chloe. Like my soul is trying to

reach out of my body and wrap itself around yours. Does that make sense?"

It does. I'm feeling the same thing.

"Yes."

He steps toward me and I wish that this damn island wasn't between us.

"Do you feel that with me?"

My core clenches and I swallow hard. It's too soon to talk about stuff like this. How can I be talking about joining souls with someone I just met?

I close my eyes and decide to just go with it. Connections like this don't happen every day and sometimes you just have to say 'fuck it' and lean into the feeling.

"I do."

He takes a breath of relief and his smile is so wide that it goes to his shining brown eyes. "That's because we're mates."

I just stare into his eyes as my whole body craves to be closer to him.

"I'm a bear shifter."

My eyes dart wide open. "You are?"

Now it all makes sense. His huge size, how he broke the thick desk so easily, his incredible strength and tremendous appetite. How did I not see it before?

"I am," he says in a deep confident voice that gets me all tingly between my legs. "And you're my mate."

It hits me hard and I grab onto the counter so I don't fall off the stool.

I've heard rumors about the intense bond that shifters have with their mates, but I never thought it would happen to me. It's like winning the love life lottery.

He walks around the counter and I look up at him as my mind swirls.

There's a bear somewhere in his chest, waiting to burst out.

"What... kind of bear?" I can barely choke the words out.

"Grizzly."

God, that's sexy. I love the idea of a huge protective beast inside of him watching out for me and having my back. It's something I've always needed.

He takes my hand and gently puts it to his hard chest.

I gasp when I feel his pec vibrating and hear the faint rumble.

"This is my bear," he says softly. "And he's mad about you."

"He is?" I'm staring at him in shock. This is all so unreal.

"Yes. And so am I."

It's a lot to take in and all of a sudden, I need some air.

I pull my hand away and rush outside before I faint on his kitchen floor.

The warm summer air feels amazing on my hot skin and I close my eyes and breathe in and out a few times, trying to take it all in and make sense of what he just told me.

But none of it makes sense. I'm just a regular poor uneducated girl who ran away from home. How can I have ended up here like this? Why do I deserve to be so lucky?

The glass door slides open a few minutes later and Ethan steps out, looking like he's going to be sick.

"Are you upset?" he asks.

"Oh, God, no," I say as I shake my head. "I'm just... overwhelmed."

He comes up to me and wraps those big delicious arms

around my shoulders. "It's overwhelming for me too," he says. "I've never wanted anything so badly in my life and I don't know how to handle all of these protective feelings I have surging through me. I don't want to share you with anyone."

I shake my head as I stare into his adoring eyes. "You don't have to."

"I'm taking care of you now, peaches," he says in a possessive voice. "You're mine now."

He claims my mouth in a hard dominant kiss that yanks the air from my lungs and makes my legs go weak.

"You belong by my side and that's exactly where you're going to stay," he says as my mind spins and I struggle to stand up from that earth-shattering kiss. "You live here now. Understand?"

I'm so happy I could die. I turn around and look at the stunning lake, amazed that I get to see it every day.

"This is my backyard?" I say as my cheeks heat up.

"It is now. Want to go out on it?"

A few minutes later, I'm sitting on the rowboat and laughing as we nearly tip over when his massive frame gets in.

It's a gorgeous mountain view, but my eyes never leave Ethan as he paddles us into the middle of the lake. The ducks quack their complaints at us before flying in the air and taking off. Now, we're truly alone. There aren't any other houses on the lake, just tall gorgeous trees with little singing birds darting through the branches.

I'm watching his big biceps flex every time he paddles and pretty soon, I'm drunk with lust and am thinking about nothing but what's hiding under that huge bulge in his pants.

"Ethan…" I say shyly. "I want to make you feel as good as you made me feel… in the shower."

His jaw clenches as he watches me.

My heart is pounding with nerves and excitement as I kneel down in front of him on the rocking boat. I slide my tingling hands along the inside of his muscular thighs, feeling his rough jeans and wishing it was his soft skin instead.

He groans when my palm reaches the thick hard outline of his erection so I add a little bit of pressure.

"*Fuck*," he hisses as I drag my hand up his long firm shaft.

My mouth is watering as I unbuckle his belt and unzip his jeans.

"Whoa!" I shout when he lifts his hips and the whole rowboat shakes violently from side to side. We both look at each other and laugh when it settles, and the nerves inside me start to melt away.

I've never done this before, but if what Ethan told me is true, he's my mate and I have nothing to worry about.

My knees ache as they dig into the hard wooden floor of the boat, but I'm only focusing on Ethan's cock as he pulls his pants and underwear down.

His cock springs free and I gulp when I see how hard it is. The sight sends a rush of heat straight to my core as I stare in awe. It's a beautiful dick all pulsing and throbbing like it's more than ready to be inside of me. It's so *thick* with a gorgeous swollen head that's covered in sticky wet pre-cum. I follow one creamy drop with my hungry eyes as it leaks out of the tiny slit at the tip and then runs down his thick veined shaft all the way to his huge balls that are swaying beneath it. They're full and swollen and look ready to stuff me full of his hot cum.

I can barely breathe as I reach out and touch it. He grits his teeth and hisses as my fingertips connect with his throbbing shaft.

The boat rocks as he sits back down on the bench, only this time neither of us are laughing.

My trembling hand wraps around it and I give his shaft a hard squeeze. More pre-cum leaks out and runs over my clenched fingers.

"Look at the mess you're making," he says in a growl. "Better lick it up with that sexy little tongue of yours."

I couldn't agree more. I lean forward and taste his salty-sweet cum, moaning at how good it feels as it fills my mouth.

He drops his head back and moans as I open my mouth wide and take the tip of his head inside. I push him in deeper and am shocked at how much his thickness stretches me.

I'm unsure of what to do, but every movement of my tongue and slide of my hand has him groaning harder and deeper, so I must be doing pretty well.

I start moving my head up and down faster, feeling him stretch out my mouth as his girth burns the back of my throat. I grip the thick root of his cock with my hand as I coat him with my saliva, loving the taste of him. My bun comes undone and my hair spills out everywhere.

"Fuck, you know how to suck your mate's cock," he growls as he pulls my loose hair to the side so he can see my lips wrapped around him.

I pull his cock out with a gasp and then start stroking his hard shaft up and down until my hand burns. My tongue is busy scooping up every drop of pre-cum leaking out, not wanting to lose any of it.

"Your mouth feels so good," he groans. "I've been

waiting for these sexy lips to wrap around my cock before you were even born. That's how long I've been waiting in torture."

His grip on my hair tightens when I take him back in my mouth.

"Just like that, peaches. Don't take me out yet. I'm going to fill your greedy throat with my hot cum. Is that what your slutty little mouth wants?"

"*Yes*," I moan with his cock pressed hard against my tongue. I take him in as far as he'll go, making my eyes water and my throat burn.

"Oh yes," he grunts, his breaths coming out fast and harsh. "Just like that. *Yes!*"

His swollen balls clench and his thick shaft throbs right before he cums deep into my mouth. I moan and cum too as I feel one hot pulsing stream of cum hit the back of my throat after another.

He jerks back violently and lets out a primal roar, sending the boat jerking to the side. I scream as it tips over and we plunge into the water.

The orgasm surging through me comes to an abrupt halt as I'm thrown under the cool lake. I kick my feet and swim back up, laughing as I look around for Ethan.

His head pops up and there's pure panic on his face as he looks around for me. When he sees that I'm safe and laughing my ass off, he starts laughing too.

The boat is tipped over and we're still giggling as we grab it and pull it back to shore.

God, this day…

Besides being nearly set on fire, it's been the most perfect day ever.

CHAPTER EIGHT

Ethan

CHLOE SAYS SOMETHING TO ME BUT I CAN'T HEAR OVER THE vicious snarling in my ears.

Claim her! CLAIM her!

My bear is out of control as he makes another wild and reckless dash to get out. *Fucking stop it!* I scream at him as I fight back his savage assault. He slips right to the surface and fights to claw his way out, hacking and shredding with all of his might to pull me back in so he can claim what's ours.

He was calm all dinner, but he's done giving me time to do it my way. The impatient fucker wants to do it his way, which I guess means marking her himself. I'll throw us both off a cliff before I let that fucking happen.

Get. The. Fuck. Back. Down! I scream at the nasty fuck.

He snaps in my ear and growls as he fights me some more.

It was going so well. I had made my specialty—honey garlic jumbo shrimps with steamed vegetables—and Chloe and I were falling in love over the nice music, the sweet wine, and the delicious food.

My grizzly's pissed that I didn't clear the table with my arm, throw her down on it, and fuck her brains out, and he's making it known.

I was in the kitchen, trying to do the dishes while Chloe cleared the table when he started in on me. I don't want her to see me like this. I'm trying to get him under control, but I'm struggling. He's never been like this before. It feels like his feral and primal strength has increased threefold since our mate walked into our lives.

Mark her! He hisses at me as he makes another charge. This time he nearly slips through, and I just manage to catch him in time, flexing my muscles so tight they're on the verge of ripping as I grit my teeth and push him back down with everything I have. We're in mid-phase. I feel the searing of my muscles growing, the tearing of skin along my spine, the dull throbbing ache as my canines extend.

I'm breathing heavily and letting out grunts as I fight him. The force slams me into the cupboards and I drop the plate in my hand. It shatters on the floor, but I don't hear anything over the brutal roaring in my ears.

He sulks back down for a second, and I try to catch my breath, knowing that this is far from over.

"Are you okay?" It's Chloe's voice, but it seems far away. "Ethan?" Through the fog in my head it sounds like I'm underwater as she calls to me.

She looks shocked—almost frightened—as she comes into the kitchen and sees me.

And I don't blame her. I must look like a monster.

The slick guy from dinner with the nice clothes and soft words is gone.

I'm leaning against the broken cupboard door, breathing like the devil's in me, and covered in sweat. My shirt is shredded from where my bear almost got out as he stretched my muscles twice their size. My hair is a mess over my wild feral eyes and I'm not sure if my teeth have gone back in by the way her eyes flash with panic when she looks at my mouth.

You stupid fuck…

I'm not sure if I'm talking to myself or to my bear. My bear for being so goddamn stubborn and ruining it all, or myself for thinking this would ever work. *What made you think that Chloe would ever want to be with a monster like you?*

My shoulders hunch over in shame and I turn away from the goddess standing in front of me. I don't deserve to look at her.

"I need a minute," I grunt as I head for the sliding doors. The broken plate cracks under my feet as I hurry outside where I can get some cover from the dark night sky.

I don't want her to see me like this. I liked how she was looking at me over dinner, with soft eyes full of interest and excitement. The look in her sweet blue eyes now… fuck, I ruined everything.

My bear snarls and starts pacing once again now that there's a wall between us and our mate. He doesn't like that I'm not with her. That possessive motherfucker doesn't know or doesn't care that he just ruined everything. He wants me to claim her over the broken plate on the kitchen floor.

Look what you did! She'll never look at us the same way again!

He growls back at me, not caring what I have to say. He's got a one-track mind and all that's on it is claim, claim, claim in an endless fucking loop.

My hands squeeze into fists and I throw my head back as he starts fighting me again. "*Stop. It,*" I hiss through gritted teeth as he slashes his way up, wrenching and tearing his way out.

I hope she's not seeing this.

My body is violently jerking around as I struggle to keep the barbaric beast contained. He's insane. I fucking hate him for ruining this for me. For us.

I'm so pissed that if I could get him out of me and wrap my hands around his thick stubborn neck, I would. Then, I wouldn't let go until his head was removed from his body and mounted over my fireplace.

My shoulders burn as they grow twice their size. Long fur sprouts out until I squeeze him back in and the long brown hairs retract back into my skin. "*Arrghh,*" I grunt as my eyes water and my teeth nearly shatter from my jaw clenching so hard. I grab two handfuls of my hair and squeeze as he fights me, snarling and gnashing his teeth as we lock horns like a couple of alphas in battle.

I crash into the railing on the balcony and that's when I see her.

Chloe is outside, watching me in front of the open door. Her hands are rubbing together nervously as she watches the horrific scene in front of her.

My bear sees the worried look in her eyes and I guess he has a shred of decency left, because he sulks back down with a grunt and lets me handle it. *Thanks, you asshole.* Like I can ever talk my way out of this.

She looks at me for a long moment as I try to catch my breath.

"What's wrong?" she finally asks in a tiny voice.

My heart sinks as I look at her, knowing my grizzly bear might have ruined everything. We could have had love. We could have had so much more.

She'll want to leave now, but I won't let her. There's no way I'm letting my mate out of my sight. But it's going to be different now. Instead of wanting to be here, I'll be forcing her to stay and that's no good when it comes to making a life together.

It's too hard to even think about and I have to look away or my heart will literally break.

Chloe hurries over to me and touches my arm. I can feel the nervous tremors in her hand and it just makes everything worse. I should be her protector. The one who takes away her fear, not gives it to her.

"You can tell me," she says in a soft voice that settles the rage in my grizzly. *Now* he's calm. *Now* he's a teddy bear. *Well, it's too fucking late*, I tell him.

She touches my cheek and my eyes start to water. "You can tell me anything," she whispers.

I swallow hard as I look into those stunning blue eyes that have already changed my life. "It's my bear… He wants you."

She doesn't turn away or run, and I love her more now than I ever have before.

"He's been waiting so long and he doesn't want to wait any longer."

Her tiny hand slides down my arm all the way to my hand. She entwines her fingers with mine and I look down at the difference. Her hand is so small and delicate, mine is enormous and pure power.

"What about you?" she asks.

My eyes dart back up to hers.

"Do you want me too?"

"More than you'll ever know," I say as my heart swells in my thundering chest. "I've never wanted anything more. You're breath in my lungs, Chloe. You're everything to me."

I take a deep breath as she watches me.

"I've been waiting too," I continue. "Thirty-six long years and every second of it has been torture without you. I'm just so happy you're here and now my bear has gone all primal and ruined it."

She shakes her head as her soft eyes bore into mine. "He hasn't ruined it."

My heart stops. "What are you saying?"

She glances back at the door as she holds onto my hand. I'm in shock as I look down at her. There's something new in her blue eyes, a sensual lust that wasn't there before.

"Come with me," she says with a deep throatiness in her voice.

My heart is pounding as she pulls me back inside.

CHAPTER NINE

Chloe

I PULL ETHAN INTO THE DARK BEDROOM AS STRONG passionate emotions run through me, making my pulse race.

The curtains are open and the view of the lake at night is stunning. The full moon is shining on the water and lighting up Ethan's dark face as I turn around to look at him.

He looks all torn up and broken. I want to soothe him and settle the beast inside.

"It's okay," I whisper as I gently touch his cheek. He's breathing fast and heavy, and I wonder if his heart is pounding as hard as mine is. "I'm yours."

He saved me, so I'm his now, to do whatever he wants with.

His sexy dark eyes are locked on me as I take a step

back and reach for my shirt. I pull it off over my head and his hungry gaze drops down to my naked breasts.

My nipples harden and begin to tingle when I see his brown eyes flash a little darker. I've never seen anything more erotic and I want him to take me so badly I can't breathe.

"I want you to have me. To *take* me."

He stands there, breathing heavily as he forcefully drags his stare away from my breasts and back up to my eyes.

"If I take you," he says in a deep dominant voice that's thick with authority and need. "I won't be able to go easy on you."

"I don't want you to go easy on me."

"I won't be able to stop until I claim every inch of you. Until I mark you."

My pussy is throbbing in anticipation. Shivers of desire begin to take over my body.

"You're my mate, Chloe, and I'm not having *anything* between us." He says it with such disdain that it brings a smile to my lips. "No pills. No condoms. I'm going to fuck you hard with my raw cock and I'm not stopping until my baby is growing in your womb. You understand me? I'm not like the other men you've been with. I can't control myself when it comes to you."

"I don't want you too." I move toward him and step up on my toes, but I still can't reach his lips. "And there hasn't been any other men. I'm a virgin. You'll be my first."

"And your last."

He swoops down and picks me up so fast that I gasp. My heart does a flip as he cradles me to his chest and kisses me so hard that my pussy begins to ache with need.

I moan as he claims my mouth with his hard demanding tongue. If this is what it feels like to be claimed by a bear shifter than I can't wait for the rest of it.

Ethan lowers me onto the bed and I moan as his lips move down my neck, giving me soft little kisses that make my body burn. His big strong hands cup my breasts and I arch my back when his mouth finally gets there. He makes me whimper when his hot tongue swirls around my hard nipples, one then the other, teasing and stroking and driving me crazy. He takes my left nipple into his mouth and sucks on it as he massages them both.

He has me practically panting at the dark sexy look in his eyes as he leans back and stares at them. No man has ever seen my naked breasts before even though plenty have tried. I'm glad I saved all of these firsts for Ethan. He deserves every single one of them. They all belong to him.

His soft luscious lips continue down my stomach as his big scratchy palms still hold onto my breasts. My hips are already writhing under him. My pussy is unbelievably wet and aching as I remember how good it felt to have his lips on it.

I gasp when he lets go of my breasts and his big hands slide down my soft stomach. I've always been shy of my stomach that never seems to go down no matter how much I exercise or how many diets I try, but Ethan doesn't seem to mind and I'm seeing my body in a new way.

"I love every inch of you," he says as he kisses my stomach in a loving way. "You're the most gorgeous creature ever created and I'm going to worship your body in the way it was meant to be worshipped by your mate."

His powerful hands grip onto the string of his shorts that I'm wearing and my heart goes into overdrive as he begins to untie the knot I made.

"I can already smell how wet your tight little virgin pussy is," he growls as he looks up at me with a heated stare. "How bad do you want your mate's hard cock?"

"So fucking bad," I moan. I don't even recognize my own voice. It's so deep and full of need.

"Good, because you're going to get it. Every long inch of it."

I lift my hips off the bed when the knot comes undone. He keeps taking long inhales, savoring the smell like a starving man savoring the smell of a bakery in the morning. My cheeks get all hot and flushed, knowing he's savoring the smell of my arousal.

With a sharp tug, he yanks the shorts down my legs and my pussy is exposed for him once again.

He sucks in a breath as he looks at it with hungry brown eyes.

"You're so wet," he says as he licks his lips. "It's all over your thighs and coating your little cunt."

I've been wet all day. I dried off after we fell into the lake, but since I had his big juicy cock in my mouth, my pussy has never stopped being wet.

This time I'm not shy. Maybe it's because he's my mate, or because we've been here before, or maybe it's because I'm so fucking turned on that the shy part of my brain is turned off for the night.

But I'm no longer timid and I want him to see *everything*.

I spread my legs wide, giving him a good look of what's his. Of what I saved for him.

My pussy was made for him—I know that now—and I want him to have it. I want him to see it. *All* of it.

Ethan lets out a low groan when he sees my pussy open for him. I can hear his bear rumbling in approval and it's incredibly sexy. The sounds go straight to my throbbing clit.

He suddenly stands up from the bed and gets undressed, but his eyes never leave my sex.

His pants and underwear come off first and then he just rips his shirt off, not bothering with the buttons and instead just tearing it to shreds.

He starts stroking his big dick and I swallow hard when I see drops of pre-cum leaking out and falling onto the hardwood floor.

I can't get over this man. He's *beautiful*.

His big arms are flexed as he slides his hand up and down his cock with long steady strokes. I can almost see his heart pounding under that massive chest of his as he gets ready to take me.

My eyes don't know where to look as my hand creeps down and I start touching myself. His hard muscles ripple and roll with every movement and I hate that I can't freeze time to take as long as I want to admire this man who is insanely, ungodly hot. The power that surrounds him is unreal.

His sculpted, chiseled abs clench and tighten as he climbs back onto the bed. He's so… fucking… *masculine*. Everything about him screams alpha male from the way he looks at me like he owns me to his possessive touch and protective stare.

He grabs my soft inner thighs with her firm fingers and spreads my legs apart even further. I'm going to have to start taking yoga if he wants me stretched out this much.

"I haven't been able to get your sweet taste out of my head all day, peaches," he says as the look on his face turns deep and seductive. "I can still taste your virgin pussy and it's making my cock so fucking hard."

My breaths start coming out rough and shallow as he slides the side of his index finger up my tingling folds.

"I'm going to claim your ripe little virgin cunt and take your cherry," he says as his mouth lowers. "But first, I want another taste of your honey…"

"*Oooh, gaaawd!*" I cry out when his mouth hits. My back arches off the bed and I grab onto the headboard behind me as he devours me *hard*.

I cum immediately, creaming all over his mouth as his tongue moves inside me. I'm shaking. I'm seeing nothing but spots dancing in front of me. My head is swirling.

And he's just getting started…

CHAPTER TEN

Ethan

My little virgin is grinding her puffy folds against my chin as I suck on her swollen clit. She just gave me an orgasm, but I want another. I'm a greedy bastard like that.

Knowing that she kept this fresh young cunt safe and intact for me is heightening everything—my arousal, my desire, and my need to claim it and make it mine for good.

My cock has cement flowing through it, I'm so hard. I want to bury it between her folds, but it's so thick and wide, and this pussy is so tight and small. I want to go in as easy as I can, and a couple of orgasms will loosen her up and help me slide inside with as little pain for her as possible.

When her body starts shaking again and she screams out as her second orgasm overtakes her, I'm ready. I grip my fat cock and move between her legs.

I rubbed her wet heat all over the lower half of my face

to keep her intoxicating scent in my nose and to keep her delicious taste in my mouth.

I've waited for so long and now the time has finally come to claim this young teenage cunt as my own.

My girl is still trembling from her orgasm as she welcomes me into her embrace. She wraps her legs around my waist as she slides her hands around my back. She's looking at me with all of the love and passion that I'm feeling in this beautiful moment.

"It's my first time too, peaches," I whisper to her.

She's still breathing heavily as she looks up at me with confusion. "First time what?"

"Doing this. All of this."

It clicks in her amazing mind.

"You're a virgin?"

I nod as I place my shaft on her mound and start grinding. She arches her back and moans.

"I wanted to wait for my mate. I wanted to wait for you."

I must sound so pathetic. I'm a thirty-six-year-old virgin for fuck's sake.

But she doesn't turn away or laugh. She arches up and presses her lips to mine, kissing me like I've never been kissed before.

I lower her back down and she falls onto the bed with our mouths still locked in a desperate and intense kiss. The room charges with heat as I reach down, grab my cock, and press the tip to her tight wet hole.

We both shudder at the same time. I can't believe how tight she is and it draws a rumble from deep in my throat. She's moaning and whimpering and I swallow each one down as I press a little further inside.

She's so fucking tight. I can't handle it.

Our mouths rip apart as all either of us can focus on is the intense feeling of our bodies connecting. Her legs tighten around me, begging for more of my length.

The warm silky walls of her pussy swallow the head of my cock and I grit my teeth as I slowly push in further. This cunt is so fresh and ripe. It's pure and ready for breeding.

Our mouths are open, our cheeks touching as we gasp in breaths of air.

I wrap my big arms around her and then thrust in hard. My cock tears through her cherry, taking her virginity forever as I give her mine.

"Hold on," she says as she clutches onto me like her life depends on it. "Just leave it in there for a second."

I'm balls deep in her little cunt and enjoying the warm feeling of her pulsing walls as they clamp down around my throbbing cock. It's the best thing I've ever felt. All those decades of torture waiting for her were worth it for this perfect moment.

My raw cock has claimed her pussy and after a few hard strokes, I'm going to claim her ripe womb.

I start grinding my hard pelvis on her clit as I hold myself inside her and she starts to cum. Her pussy tightens even more around me as she screams into my ear. I hiss through my clenched teeth as she squeezes me impossibly tight. I'm close to cumming too.

When her frantic cries die down and her orgasm starts to dissipate, her pussy begins to loosen up a little. It's still deathly tight, but it allows me to start rocking in and out slowly.

Her hips move to my rhythm and soon, I'm sliding in and out with full deep strokes.

I've claimed her cunt, but I haven't marked her and

this irks my sleeping bear. He starts to get antsy and irritated as I fuck her.

Mark her!

Shut up, I warn him. This is *our* moment. Chloe and mine. I'm not going to let him ruin it.

Mark her. NOW!

But the fucker always insists on ruining everything.

She's in enough pain from my cock. I don't want to sink my teeth into her neck. Not now. Not during our first time. I've caused her too much pain already and I'm not strong enough to cause her any more.

My bear doesn't like this answer and he surges forward when I'm mid-thrust. The savage beast snarls as he mauls his way forward in a savage rush to the surface. I let out a roar as I tighten my body to hold him back.

It barely works, but I do manage to shove him back just in time. He hovers at the surface as I flex my muscles trying to keep him away from her.

I squeeze my eyes shut, fighting as he starts to slip through. *What the fuck are you doing?* I scream at him, but he doesn't fucking care. He wants his mark on her now and he's not taking fuck you for an answer.

He bursts forward in another frantic surge and I grit my teeth and grunt. I'm barely hanging onto control as I thrust my hips faster, fucking her even harder.

My arms burn as they begin to swell and grow. My back balloons in size as my canines ache as they extend. I fuck her harder and faster to distract her from the freakshow happening above her. I force my eyes open and look down at her and see nothing but heavy lust in her eyes as she watches me. She's into this.

She's moaning and rocking her hips, meeting my cock

with every hard thrust. Her tiny hands run up my arms and her not-so-tiny nails dig deep into my biceps.

I'm still struggling with my wild grizzly as I make her pussy mine. He's trying to claw his way to the surface and I know that my eyes must be glowing a bright golden color right now. My teeth must be pressing against my lips, making me look half animal.

I wanted to be an animal in bed for my mate, but not literally.

My body swells more and I know that my skin is about to tear. It's pulled tight across every swollen muscle. I'm holding it back with everything I have as I slide in and out of her.

"Fuck," I grunt as my fingertips split and long black nails slide out. They cut right through the sheets and dig into the mattress that's jerking back and forth with every hard pump of my hips.

"*Do it,*" she moans as her tits lurch up and down with every frantic thrust. "Whatever you need to do. I can take it."

I have no restraint left. I can't fight the crushing desires ripping though my body any longer. My mouth moves to her neck and I lick her soft tender flesh. I pull back my tingling lips and drag my sharp canines along the supple skin over her collarbone.

"I want it," she moans as she lifts her chin up and away, tightening the skin on her neck for me. "Do it. *Please.*"

My cock is sliding in and out of her wet cunt as I press my two extended teeth to her skin and then plunge them in, biting and marking her as my own. Forever.

The sweet coppery taste of her blood fills my mouth as she whimpers and cries, taking it like a champ. Just before the mark is complete, her pussy erupts around my cock and she cums hard.

A warm rush of her hot juices surges down my long shaft and oozes out onto my swollen balls. Her pulsing cunt tightens around me and I let go of her neck and of my orgasm with a roar.

She holds onto me tightly as I bury myself within her and unload every drop of my cum deep inside her hot pulsing cunt.

The heat sweeping through me is like nothing I've ever experienced before and it overtakes me in the most delicious way.

My bear retreats down inside, happy and content. The fucking asshole.

I can't stay mad at him now. I'm too damn happy and without his stubborn insistence, my mark wouldn't be on my mate's neck. Now, every shifter who sees her will know that she belongs to Ethan Sullivan.

Every human male who sees her will get uneasy and look away. They won't understand why, but deep down they'll instinctually know that this ripe young girl is taken and that looking at her could be fatal.

Chloe whimpers when I slide my hard cock out of her and drop onto the bed. I look down at my dick and grin when I see it covered in her cream and virginity. I wish I could keep it like this forever. I never want to wash it off.

She rolls over and drapes her arm and leg on my body. Her sweet breath is tickling my bicep as she runs her hand up and down my chest.

"I'm yours now?" she asks softly.

I'm still breathing heavily from my orgasm. "Yeah."

"And your bear is happy?"

"*Very* happy."

"Good." She rests her head on my shoulder and I'm still having a hard time believing that all this is real. "I like being yours."

"That's good," I say as I hold her tight. "Because you always will be."

CHAPTER ELEVEN

Chloe

I'VE BEEN NAKED FOR FOUR DAYS.

Every time I try to put some clothes on, Ethan rips it off and has sex with me. It's like he's doing it just to spite me because he likes to see me naked. But who am I to complain?

I'm in the bathroom hiding from him. My pussy is so sore from the constant use over the last few days. Three times this morning alone.

He bangs on the door before I can even put the toothpaste on the new brush he gave me.

"Why is the door closed?" His possessive voice booms through the door as I start to brush.

"Because I'm using the bathroom," I shout back with a grin on my lips. This man is obsessed with me. I *love* it.

"I can hear you brushing your teeth."

"Damn," I curse under my breath.

"I heard that too. I'm coming in."

I turn to him with a grin as the door swings open and his huge body squeezes through the frame.

"I don't like doors between us," he says as he looks my naked body up and down.

My pussy starts tingling and heating up from the hungry look in his eyes. Maybe it's not *that* sore. I could go one more time.

I look at his crotch and shake my head when I see his cock hardening as he walks over. This man is *relentless*. He doesn't stop. I'd swear he was a rabbit shifter with the way he goes at it.

He stands right behind me and grabs my bare hips with his strong hands. This *really* gets me wet.

I narrow my eyes at him through the mirror.

"What do you think you're doing?" I ask him with the toothbrush in my mouth.

"I want to feel your pussy cumming on my cock," he growls in a low gravelly voice.

"Again?" I ask, staring at him in disbelief.

He groans. "It's been so long."

"It's been twenty minutes!"

"Exactly."

I try not to laugh as I continue brushing my teeth. "Well, I'm busy now, so you're just going to have to wait."

"Fine." He drops to his knees behind me and I whip my head around with a gasp.

"What are you doing???"

His big hands cup my ass cheeks and he lifts them and spreads them apart. "Waiting."

Before I can answer, he dives in, licking and sucking from my clit that's now throbbing all the way up to my asshole. This man is shameless. He's insatiable. I think I'm in love.

The moans start flying out of me and I forget all about my dental hygiene. The toothbrush falls to the sink with a clatter as I press my ass against him, wanting more of his hot mouth on me.

After I cum once, he stands up and slides his cock inside, taking me doggystyle over the sink. I stare at him through the mirror while he thrusts in and out of me until we're both screaming out.

Later, when we're panting on the floor, I turn to him.

"I need some clothes."

"No."

I laugh. God, he can be so frustrating.

"So, I'm just going to be naked for the rest of my life?"

"Sounds good to me."

"What about in winter?"

"I'll keep you warm."

My eyes narrow on him. "Ethan."

His narrow back on me. "Chloe."

"I need my clothes. And some of my things."

I'm laughing, but he looks genuinely concerned.

"I don't want you to leave. I don't like you out there in the world."

"Then come with me."

"Oh, I'm coming with you," he quickly says. "That's for sure."

I laugh again. He's so possessive it borders on being barbaric.

"Come on," I say as I get off the floor. "Let's go to my place and get my stuff. Then we'll go get some groceries and stop for lunch."

He looks tense. Uneasy.

"What?" I ask him.

"There will be guys there."

"So?"

"They'll be looking at you."

I laugh. Is this guy for real?

"Guys have looked at me before."

A flash of anger crosses his face and I see his hand squeeze into a fist. I take his hand, open it up, and lace my fingers through his.

"It will be fine," I tell him in a soft comforting voice. "If anyone looks at me for more than two seconds, you can growl at them. Okay?"

"More than one second."

I smile. "Deal."

"You play tennis?" Ethan asks when he spots my tennis racket in my closet.

"Once in a while," I say as I pack my clothes into the open suitcase on my bed.

"At the tennis courts?"

"That's usually where one plays tennis, yeah."

"And there are guys there? Watching you?"

I grin as I shake my head. I didn't realize how possessive bear shifters got when their mates were in public. I kinda like it. I've never had anyone looking out for me before and it feels nice.

"I play at an all women's court," I lie, just to make him feel better. It works. I smile when I see the look of relief on his face.

He continues snooping around my apartment and I

grin as I watch him. I like having him in my place. He makes it look so tiny.

When I have everything I need, Ethan takes my suitcase and we head back downstairs. I don't know when the next time I'll be back will be, but something tells me there might be snow on the ground.

He puts the suitcase into the back of his pickup truck, lifting it as easily as if it were empty. I take one last look at my small apartment that I rent over the garage of my landlord's house and smile. I've been here for two years and it was the only place that's ever felt like home. Well, the only place since I've been staying at Ethan's house. That feels like my real home now.

I glance across the street and notice a man sitting in a black car watching us. He quickly looks away when I make eye contact with him, and then starts his car and leaves.

Something doesn't feel right about it and there's an empty pit in my stomach as I watch him drive off.

The worrying feeling disappears as Ethan steps up behind me and wraps his big possessive arms around my shoulders. How can I be afraid of anything with this protective beast looking out for me?

"Ready for lunch?" I ask him. "I'm starving."

"Are you sure you don't want to do take-out and eat at home?"

I roll my eyes and laugh.

"Let's go," I say as I grab his hand and pull him to the truck. "We're eating at the restaurant!"

CHAPTER TWELVE

Chloe

I'M ENJOYING THE SUNSET ON THE BALCONY WHEN ETHAN walks out with two big mojitos. This man can do it all.

He has lots of vacation time saved up over the three years he's been a fireman and he's decided to take a big chunk of it now. And since I'm on a permanent vacation from my job after my boss tried to kill me and burn the place down, we have all the time in the world to be together.

"Cheers," he says as we clink glasses and enjoy the view.

His jaw is a little tight, which usually happens when he's worrying about something. I love that I'm already getting to know all of his mannerisms and ticks. It's only been a few days, but I already feel like I know him so well.

"What's the matter?" I ask after I take a sip of the deliciously minty drink.

"Nothing," he grunts.

"You're lying." His eyes snap down to mine. "Please don't lie to me. Ever."

"It was just… I saw a car on our way back from the restaurant."

"The restaurant where you made a big scene about having a male waiter and made them move us into a girl's section? That restaurant?"

I'm grinning as he shakes his head, trying not to laugh. "Yeah. That's the one."

"Okay. What about this car?"

"I got the sense he was following us."

My stomach drops when I remember the guy from earlier. "Was it a black car?"

His eyes dart open. "How did you know?"

"With a man inside?"

"Chloe, who was that man?"

"I don't know, but I saw him waiting outside my apartment. He took off when I looked at him."

Ethan's big biceps start quivering as he turns back to the lake with a fierce glare. "I knew I should have stopped and pulled him through his windshield."

"Do you think he works for… Aylwin Kirk?" Just saying his name makes the tiny hairs on the back of my neck stand up.

I've been too busy enjoying and discovering Ethan that I haven't been thinking of him much. But now it all comes crashing back to me. The cold look in Mr. Kirk's grey eyes when he pulled me to the floor and handcuffed me. The way he just walked out without a care in the world as I begged and screamed for him to let me loose. The smoke. The fire. Then, Ethan.

"He tried to kill you for a reason," Ethan says. "Were

you in the wrong spot at the wrong time or do you know too much?"

"Probably both."

Ethan huffs out a breath as his forearm flexes. I jump as the glass in his hand explodes. "I'll kill him for even thinking about hurting you."

I drop my eyes, watching the ice cubes slide on the wooden deck as the drink and mint leaves disappear through the cracks.

"I must be too dangerous to him," I say, more to myself than to Ethan. "I was his secretary. I knew everything. Appointment times, dates, who he met with, who he sent money too. I mailed the checks."

Ethan stomps back toward the door. "I'm going to make a call."

"To who?"

"A friend in town," he says as he grabs the sliding door and rips it open. "Sheriff Austin Peters. Maybe he can find this guy so I can end his life."

He storms into the house and I just stare at the calm lake as my insides churn. This is not good. I don't want Ethan going up against Mr. Kirk. What if he gets hurt? Or worse?

God, I can't even think about it. I close my eyes and take a couple of deep breaths.

When it does nothing to calm me, I open my eyes and gasp when I see an enormous grey bird in the sky.

I narrow my eyes on it and watch in confusion as it plummets out of the sky in the distance, getting bigger by the second.

"Ethan!" I call out to him as the nerves in my belly start to go nuts. "Come see this bird. It's huge!"

Ethan rushes out a second later and wraps his protective arms around me when he sees it.

"That's no bird," he says as he pulls me inside. "That's a dragon."

My mouth drops.

"A *what?!?*"

CHAPTER THIRTEEN

Ethan

MY BEAR GETS READY TO ROCK AS THE GREY DRAGON COMES swooping down over the lake. My grizzly charges to the surface, snarling and snapping his teeth, and for once I'm happy I have a fierce grumpy bastard of a bear inside me.

Chloe looks pale and terrified as I shove her inside the house and slam the door closed. I want to take her in my arms and tell her she's safe. Tell her that I won't let anyone or anything ever hurt her, but I have bigger dragons to fry.

I quickly climb up the stone wall of my house and stand on the roof as he comes. He heads straight for me and my heart pounds in excitement as I wait. I've been waiting to make this guy pay for touching my girl for too long. Well, the wait is over.

I grit my teeth and flex my arms as I glare at him. His huge jaws open and just as he arrives over my house, he lets out a ball of fire that surges toward me. I leap over it and grab onto his scaly foot, pulling him down as he tries to rise. My feet leave the burning roof as he struggles to fly higher with my heavy body weighing him down.

"She's *my* girl," I hiss as I reach up and try to grab his wing. My fingers graze it and my body swings back down when I'm unable to grab a hold of it.

My inner grizzly is chomping in my ear, desperate to get out. He'll get his turn, but first, I want my taste. I want this guy to feel my wrath.

I time the flapping of his wing and when it swings back down, I lurch back up and grab the tip. This time I get a hold of it and yank it down.

The dragon lets out a chirping roar as we start spinning downward like a helicopter with the tail shot out. "No!" I gasp when I see the fire spreading on the roof of my house. Chloe is inside.

Panic starts to fill me as we crash through the trees, snapping branches and breaking trunks before we land hard on the ground. The air is knocked out of my lungs and I can't breathe as I look around for the dragon. He's pinned between two trees and can't move.

"Alright, you furry motherfucker," I tell my bear as I push up to my knees. "You've been a savage bastard my whole life. Now, it's time to make it all worth it. It's time for you to shine."

I let the beast loose and he comes roaring out. He explodes out of me, pissed and ready to defend what's ours.

I watch from inside as he lets out a deafening roar and charges at the dragon.

CHAPTER FOURTEEN

Chloe

I'M GETTING A SERIOUSLY BAD CASE OF DÉJÀ VU AS THE HOUSE fills with smoke. I run outside and frantically look around for Ethan, but he's nowhere to be seen.

It hits me even more how much I love him and I don't know what I'm going to do with myself if something happens to him. Ethan told me all about mates and how happily ever after the couples live after they bond, but what about when one of them dies? He didn't say anything to me about that. About the extreme heartbreak. The intense loneliness. The feeling of wanting to die because you know you'll never find anything even remotely similar to what you had.

Stop, Chloe. Don't start spiraling, you have shit to do!

I look up at the roof and curse when I see the flames spreading along it. This place has felt like home over the past few days and I can't watch it burn.

I rush into the house with my heart hammering in my chest and head straight to the phone. I call 911 and ask the girl who answers named Kinsley to send the fire department over as soon as possible.

After that, I run back outside and grab the hose on the side of the house. I turn it on and try to spray the water onto the flames, but it's spreading so fast and the water can't reach much higher than the side of the house.

That's when I hear the fighting. The sounds are so vicious that they make my legs weak with terror. I know the savage roaring is Ethan's bear. I know he's fighting for me, but I still hate that he's going through this right now and I hate even more that I'm the cause of it. I've been nothing but trouble for him since I walked into his life.

The horrible sounds get louder and more vicious as the two animals go at it. I can't see them, but I can see the tops of the trees shaking where they are.

My eyes are glued to the spot for what feels like hours when suddenly, Aylwin's dragon comes bursting through the trees into the air.

"Oh my God!" I shout as my hand flies to my mouth. Ethan's grizzly bear is on top of him, clutching onto the back of the dragon's neck with his powerful jaws. The rest of his body is hanging down and I can't breathe as they go higher and higher. If he falls from that height, he'll surely die.

When they get over the lake, the weight of the bear becomes too much for the dragon or maybe the blood he's losing from the wound on his neck is making him weaker, but he begins to fall. With Ethan still holding on.

The two plummet as my stomach sinks and then they crash hard into the water, making a giant splash as they disappear down below.

It feels like an eternity goes by as I wait there with my chest burning for him to come up.

"Oh thank God!" I whisper when I see his human head emerge from the water. But my spirits get kicked back down when Aylwin's human head emerges as well.

Ethan's protective eyes search me out and then lock onto me when he sees me standing on the balcony in front of his burning house. He starts swimming in a full sprint toward me as Aylwin follows close behind.

I run down to the water to meet him, but he's shaking his head in a panic as he runs up onto the shore, waving me away. "No! Run, Chloe! Run!"

He's naked in the waist-deep water and there are long claw marks along his chest that are seeping out blood. I don't want to leave him. If he dies then I want to die too. I don't want to be on this planet without him.

"I'm not leaving you," I tell him and the look on his face is half love, half disappointment. Love that I'm staying with him until the end no matter what and disappointment that the end for both of us might be soon.

The look doesn't last long because he turns around just as Aylwin leaps onto him. Ethan catches him in the air, turns, and slams him into the water. I wince as Ethan throws devastating punches that land with hard thuds.

Aylwin wraps his arm around Ethan's leg and pulls him down and I scream as he disappears underwater. I grab a baseball-sized rock from the shore and throw it at Aylwin with all my might. It hits him in the head and he turns to me with a vicious sneer.

"You're hardly worth all of this trouble," he hisses at me. "Once I kill your mate in front of you, I'll bend you over to see what's got this bear all worked up. I hardly doubt even *that* will be worth any of this."

Ethan leaps out of the water, grabs Aylwin by the neck, and snarls in his face. "That's the *last* time you talk to my mate!"

Aylwin's eyes go wide as Ethan chokes the air out of him. His hands start clawing at Ethan's wrist in desperation as my protective mate starts to punch him in the face with his free hand.

The sound of a firetruck siren fills the air and gets louder by the second. I turn to run back and meet them, but my body freezes when I see the house engulfed in flames.

It doesn't matter, I tell myself as my hands begin to shake. *All that matters is we survive and end up together.*

I grit my teeth and start sprinting to meet the truck. The heat from the flames is so intense that some of the trees around the house have caught on fire as well.

"What happened?" the fire chief asks as he jumps down from the rolling truck. "Where's Ethan?"

"Come!" I shout in a desperate tone as I run back to the lake. The four of them run after me.

"Is this chick a pyromaniac or something?" I hear one of them ask another as we run.

I guess that's fair. Every time they see me, I am surrounded by fire.

"Oh shit," one of them says as we run past the house. "Is that a dragon shifter I smell."

"In the lake," I shout as I point to where Ethan and Aylwin are exchanging devastating blows. Aylwin is free from Ethan's chokehold and is getting the upper hand. I hate that I'm the cause of all this.

The four firefighters run into the water and jump on top of my old boss. Violent waves ripple out from the brawl as the four guys each grab a limb and hold Aylwin down.

Ethan steps up to him, breathing hard and looking mean as hell. His flexed shoulders are hunched up and his arms look impossibly jacked as he bears down on the man who dared to touch his mate.

"You never touch a mated girl," Ethan hisses as he stands over him. "Especially mine."

I turn away with a wince as my protector grabs a hold of his head and breaks his neck.

Aylwin slumps down into the water dead.

It's over. Almost.

There's still a fire to put out.

The boys run back to the truck to take care of Ethan's house as he comes up to me looking bloody and bruised and sexier than ever.

"You nearly died for me," I tell him as he comes up to me, towering over my body. "You killed for me."

"I'd do anything for you," he says in a voice that's full of love and tenderness. "You're my girl, peaches. Nothing else matters but you."

The firehoses burst to life as the boys start to douse the flames that have ruined his home.

"Your house..." I say as tears start to fill my eyes.

He cups my cheek and wipes the tears from my face.

"We'll build a new one." He doesn't look upset at all. It's like everything he needs is standing right in front of him. "It will be *our* house. We'll start fresh. A new house with lots of rooms for all of the cubs I'm going to breed into you."

I grin as I gaze into his protective eyes. "I love you, Ethan."

He wraps his arms around me and kisses the top of my

head. "I love you too, peaches. It's all blue skies and rainbows from here on out."

I look up at his face that I'm already obsessed with and smile.

I'm pretty sure he's right.

EPILOGUE

Chloe

Seven months later…

"EXCITED?" ETHAN ASKS ME AS HE COVERS MY EYES WITH HIS big hands.

"So excited," I say with my heart racing as he carefully guides me into our new house.

We rebuilt it bigger and better on the same spot on the lake. Ethan insisted on having at least six bedrooms. I insisted on knowing what for.

He just smiled and quickly changed the subject. My stomach is already round with our first child—a boy—and I think I have to get used to it. This man has big plans for my womb. That's okay, I love being pregnant with his child.

"Careful of the cargo," he says as his big protective hand cradles my baby bump away from something. "Keep your eyes closed!"

"I am!" I lie as I try to peek through his thick fingers, but it's impossible. His hand is so damn big.

He guides me past the master bedroom to the room on the left.

"Can I open now?" I ask him. "We're going to have guests over soon."

"You know I took care of everything," he says as he holds onto me. You'd swear I was bedridden by the way he does everything for me when in actuality, the pregnancy is going great. Our little cub is six months old with a flawless bill of health.

The house was ready last week and we just moved in two days ago. I've seen it all except for this room, which Ethan has forbidden me to see. He wanted it to be a surprise and he was so excited that I couldn't deny him. Besides, I've been so tired lately with the move that I just let him do whatever he wanted with it.

I was sad to leave my old apartment where we've been staying this entire time, but the landlords weren't too upset to see us go. We have been a little loud during the nights, and the mornings...

...and sometimes the afternoons.

Okay, most afternoons.

"All right," he says as he releases my eyes. "Open."

"Oh, Ethan," I say as my heart swells inside my chest. He set up the most adorable little baby's room with soft pastel blues and plush teddy bears all over the place. "I can't believe you did this."

I turn around and look into his loving eyes, wondering how I got so lucky.

He's a big, rough, mean-looking guy, but inside he's a real softie. Especially when it comes to me and our growing little cub. I can't wait to see him as a father.

"Are you happy?" he asks.

I stand up on my toes and he leans down so I can kiss him. "Thrilled. He's going to be so happy here."

"*We're* going to be so happy here."

I let him wrap his big arms around me as I look at the room, feeling the excitement build inside. "We are. Starting now."

$\sim$

I love it when the guys from the firehouse get together. It's always so much fun.

"First, you find a mate," Carter says as he shakes his head at Ethan. "Now, you're having a kid. Why do you keep insisting on ruining your life?"

Ethan just laughs at him. "You don't know what you're missing, Carter. Life has no spark without a mate."

I grin as I watch Carter shake his head. He's really hot (not that I'd ever tell Ethan that—he'd kill the poor guy) with tattoos all over his muscular arms and chest. The guy could get any girl he wants, but for some reason, he's not interested in any of them.

I'd love for him to meet the right girl and have to eat his words one day, but who knows if that will ever happen? There are four beautiful fit bear shifters here who still haven't found the girls for them.

Maybe it's time I start helping them look…

Something tells me I won't be the only girl hanging around the firehouse for long.

Once one bear finds their mate, it catches like wildfire, passing from one shifter to the next.

I grin as I look around the room full of hot eligible fire-fighting bachelors.

I wonder who will be next?

EPILOGUE

Chloe

Eight years later…

I WAKE UP WITH A GROAN AND REACH OVER TO FIND AN empty bed. My eyes fly open and instead of seeing Ethan's gorgeous sleeping face or broad muscular back facing me, I see the floor-to-ceiling window with the stunning view of our private lake.

It's a beautiful end of spring day and I take a couple of minutes to admire the gorgeous water as our only neighbors—six cute ducks—glide along the glassy surface.

The trees are starting to sprout their leaves and I wake up with a smile knowing that summer is right around the corner.

Nine o'clock?!?

It's not even Mother's Day and Ethan has let me sleep in. He's the best.

I don't hear any of our kids fighting or yelling or running around, so he must have taken them out, which means that I have a few quiet minutes to myself.

Not wanting to waste them laying in bed, I get up and rush over to the kitchen. The place is spotless and I already have a big grin on my face when I see the full pot of coffee waiting for me. There's a note with a gorgeous yellow flower resting on it and I immediately head over to see what it says.

Ethan is always leaving me love notes in my purse or car, or my favorite—on the steam in the mirror whenever I take a shower.

I take my time and smell the carnation, savoring the moment and knowing how much I'm loved by my big burly bear shifter mate.

Thoughts of Ethan and how he spoiled me in bed last night are swirling through my mind as I pour a coffee and take the note over to the couch.

You, my love, are more desirable than a cup of morning coffee

- Love your possessive mate

I laugh as I put it in my pocket to add to the box with the thousands of others he's left me over the years.

The lake looks too tempting, so after my coffee, I head outside, grab my kayak, and lug it down to the water.

Ethan gave it to me last Christmas and I absolutely

love it. It's the best way to start the morning. Well, second-best after having Ethan between my legs.

I'm paddling across the lake and when I get to the middle, I spot my papa bear coming out of the woods with my four little cubs beside him.

Ethan's protective bear spots me immediately and he doesn't take his eyes off me.

"Good morning!" I shout to my cubs who take a little longer to find me. When they do they rush into the water and start swimming over.

Ethan goes in last, but he quickly passes them and arrives at my kayak first. His bear is all grunts and snorts as he swims circles around my kayak.

"Thanks for the wonderful morning," I whisper as I ruffle my hand through the fur on top of his head as he swims by. "I'd choose you over my morning coffee too."

My little grizzly cubs catch up and soon I have five bears swimming around me. I pet each one of them and each one brings a smile to my heart. I love my furry family so much it hurts.

"Let's head home," I tell them, "and I'll make everyone chocolate chip pancakes with whipped cream."

This gets their attention and my four little ones head straight for our house. Ethan stays right beside me as I begin to paddle home.

My protective bear likes to keep me close by.

I smile as I watch him trying to swim straight while he keeps his eyes on me, and a couple of times, I accidentally smack him in the head with the paddle when he strays too close.

He doesn't seem to mind. I seem to be able to do no wrong when it comes to him.

Parker, my oldest, is the first one onshore. Then Amelia, Jake, and then my youngest, Jessica.

One by one, they phase back into their human forms and then race up the steps into the house to get a seat at the table.

My furry grizzly chaperone looks over at me and I smile at the amazing world we've built together.

I cherish the past, I'm excited for the future, and I'm ready to start another amazing day with my little furry family.

The End!

Our firefighting bear shifters will return in

Drawn to the Alpha
Book Two in the *Alphas in Heat* series

DON'T BE SHY. COME FOLLOW ME...

I WON'T BITE UNLESS YOU ASK ME TO

Olivia T. Turner's complete list of books can be found at:

www.OliviaTTurner.com

amazon.com/author/oliviatturner

facebook.com/OliviaTTurnerAuthor

instagram.com/authoroliviatturner

goodreads.com/OliviaTTurner

amazon.com/author/oliviatturner

bookbub.com/authors/olivia-t-turner

AUDIOBOOKS

Check out my complete collection of audiobooks at
www.OliviaTTurner.com!

I'm adding more of your favorite OTT stories all the time!

BARE FOR THE ALPHA

THE RIDGE BROTHERS BEAR SHIFTERS BOOK ONE

I'm new in this Montana shifter town and no one will even
so much as glance in my direction.
My father has made sure of that.
He's the Sheriff and he's got three rules:
1. Don't talk to my daughter.

2. No fighting between crews.

3. See rule #1.

I'm all alone and wishing for someone to look my way.

And then someone does.

A mean looking grizzly bear shifter named Damon Ridge, and once he sees me, he refuses to look away.

This rough, wild-looking man keeps telling me I'm his mate.

He keeps saying he's going to claim me.

That I belong to him.

I didn't realize how *possessive* a bear shifter could get.

If I knew how *obsessed* these huge men could be, I never would have come here.

But now that I know how it feels, I'm never going to leave…

Get it at www.OliviaTTurner.com

Printed in Great Britain
by Amazon